About the Author

Tina Ridlon lives with her husband in Bridgton, ME. Spirit Cooking is her first published work.

Spirit Cooking: Art as Metaphor

Tina Ridlon

Spirit Cooking: Art as Metaphor

Olympia Publishers
London

www.olympiapublishers.com
OLYMPIA PAPERBACK EDITION

Copyright © Tina Ridlon 2023

The right of Tina Ridlon to be identified as author of
this work has been asserted in accordance with sections 77 and 78 of
the Copyright, Designs and Patents Act 1988.

All Rights Reserved

No reproduction, copy or transmission of this publication
may be made without written permission.
No paragraph of this publication may be reproduced,
copied or transmitted save with the written permission of the publisher,
or in accordance with the provisions
of the Copyright Act 1956 (as amended).

Any person who commits any unauthorized act in relation to
this publication may be liable to criminal
prosecution and civil claims for damage.

A CIP catalogue record for this title is
available from the British Library.

ISBN: 978-1-80439-371-0

This is a work of fiction.
Names, characters, places and incidents originate from the writer's
imagination. Any resemblance to actual persons, living or dead, is
purely coincidental.

First Published in 2023

Olympia Publishers
Tallis House
2 Tallis Street
London
EC4Y 0AB

Printed in Great Britain

Dedication

For Nanny – because you were the first to believe. And for Scott – the light and love of my life.

Acknowledgements

Thank you to Marina Abramovic for your work that has changed the world.

A white room. In its center a simple wooden table and two hard backed wooden chairs. A woman sits at the table, hands in her lap and head bowed as if in prayer. She wears a long red dress, the color startling in the plain room. Her body is still and patient. She is calm. She breathes in, she breathes out. She waits.

A middle aged man with silver blending through ink colored hair steps apart from the people waiting on the periphery. He crosses to the middle of the room and fills the empty chair across the table from the woman wearing the red dress. She senses his presence and one sees her inhale deeply and slowly, as if to settle herself, before lifting her head to meet his eyes with her own. Her gaze is open and gentle. The stranger looking back at her holds her stare with inquisitive and questioning depths.

An indeterminate amount of time passes in this way, a gaze shared between strangers seeing each other for the first time. Their voices are silent, no words are needed or wanted in this space. She looks at him, unblinking and still, and he looks back. After a while the man stands and walks away, returning to the sidelines, becoming part of the watching and curious crowd once again.

The woman still at the table lowers her head and closes her eyes. Minutes later another stranger will cross the empty space to sit at this table and she will lift her head, meet their eyes with her soft and steady gaze, and she will give wordlessly of herself for as long as needed.

The year is 2010. The woman's name is Marina Abramovic. For seventy-five days Marina sat in this room at MoMA for eight hours a day, giving her presence completely to anyone who wanted to sit with her, however long they wished. The series is titled 'The Artist is Present' and continues to be a powerful performance of art made flesh.

***

I wasn't in New York in 2010. I never stepped inside the Museum of Modern Art or saw Marina Abramovic sitting at that table. I wasn't there to experience the energy felt in that white room, to see the thousands who waited hours in line to sit with the artist, to share in conversation with those who gathered day after day just to observe.

I have watched several video clips of the performance and I have seen photos of the ones who participated in this form of living art and I know that I have been changed by it despite the distance and despite the many years that have passed since 'The Artist is Present' took place.

I saw tears falling over faces both young and older. I saw eyes haunted and hurting, looking to be truly seen. I saw a raw nakedness of emotion that is rarely seen between strangers. I saw acceptance, admiration, openness and fear in the eyes of the ones who took that place at the table and reflected back to them I saw kindness and empathy.

Connection.

That is, I believe, what so many were seeking. In a broken and hurting world there is a wounded and scarred and disfigured humanity that exists in an atmosphere of isolation, longing for connection and validation.

I like to believe that is what so many experienced in their time with Marina. The willingness of one person to shed the constraints of time and movement and to just be with another, fully present and fully aware in a shared time and space, has an impact on one's soul.

Watching video of the performance on the web I felt that it

was one of the most powerful things I have seen. I felt awe at the range of emotions people felt without a single word having been spoken. I felt drawn to see more and more of this from an unidentifiable feeling it brought out in me. I felt a wetness fill my eyes that threatened to run over. I felt the power of silence to bring closeness instead of separation. The difference laid in conscientious awareness. Being physically mentally and emotionally in the present moment.

I imagined myself in that room with the table and Marina and the empty seat and I wondered if I would have had the courage to sit with her. What would it have felt like to be seen by her? To look into her tired but kind eyes that had experienced so much in the world and know that she was simply requiring me to be still with her? Would I have experienced the same emotions as a participant that I had as a distant observer?

I thought about the meaning in this work and how to interpret the performance as a whole. Was the artist using her body to reflect to the world humanity's hunger for connection? Was she a silent invitation to experience living in the present instead of dwelling on what has become past and a constant looking ahead? Was her intention to allow those who felt insignificant and lost a chance to be fully seen as they are without pretention?

Beyond meaning and interpretation I wondered at a person's ability to sit in stillness and quiet for so long. The physical discomfort Marina must have experienced in all those hours over seventy-five days. The strength of mind it must take to resist that discomfort and to remain unflinchingly present with each strange face before her.

I think of it as a reflection of a cultural inability to strip away differences, judgments and facades; to show in a powerful way the innate need for a connection that encompasses humanity as a whole but is, at the same time, so deeply lacking.

***

The earth's rotation around the sun has again roused nature from its winter dormancy. The sun feels closer and warmer and there are signs of spring awakening as I walk the streets of downtown.

I am still thinking of Marina Abramovic and The Artist is Present.

I am not walking simply to enjoy the warmth or for exercise. I walk methodically and observantly with a purpose, taking in the people around me and trying an exercise in being fully present in the moment. This is harder than I imagined it would be as my mind wanders over and around many thoughts at once like a meandering brook.

I pass an elderly man in a button down cardigan with a wooden cane, his eyes cast down to the brick sidewalk as we pass one another.

I listen to the flow of traffic; an occasional impatient horn interrupting the sounds of tires on tarmac.

There is the aroma of ground coffee beans as I near the coffee bar. A younger woman stands outside the entrance mid-conversation on her phone. Her eyes briefly glance over me as I am walking past her but I know that she doesn't really see me, her attention focused on the person listening.

I approach the intersection and join the people at the crosswalk who are waiting for the Walk light to signal. I observe the impassive expressions of their waiting. Some are looking ahead at the signal light. Some are busy looking at phones in their hands. Most are somewhere else entirely although they are standing here waiting.

I cross the street and turn left around a corner where there is a popular pizzeria. A man sits on an overturned plastic crate smoking a cigarette. He wears a black shirt with the logo of the pizza shop in white lettering and a sauce stained apron. He glances up as I walk by and with a curt nod of acknowledgement in my direction he goes back to smoking.

A woman out for a run with earbuds playing in her ears and her gaze focused on the path ahead.

A group of teens at a park bench, laughing and talking and sipping from aluminum soda cans, oblivious to passersby.

I walk and walk and take in the people I see. It is hard not to notice the silence of strangers, the palpable disconnect between them, and I wonder when this became a learned behavior. I wonder why it has only now become so obvious to me.

I read once that after 9/11 people had set up small tables on sidewalks and were available to the public to sit with and be listened to. People would come and sit and share their stories of grief and loss and shock with complete strangers. There was a sense of desperation among the crowds; a need to feel connected to one another, to be united through a shared experience.

I wonder why it is only after a tragedy that there is a need for connection and unity? Is it only through devastation that humanity is awakened to truly see one another?

***

The year is 1974. A performance art in Naples, Italy titled 'Rhythm 0'.

A long table draped with a white cloth. On top of the table are placed simplistic objects that are pleasing to the senses like honey, a rose, feathers, perfume, candles and a polaroid camera.

There are other objects that inflict pain and hurt, like whips, chains, knives, razor blades, a pistol and a single bullet.

Seventy-two objects in total; half pleasurable and half painful.

Marina Abramovic stands at the front of the room. Her instructions to her audience are simple: for six hours they can choose any object from the table and do to her body what they wish. She will stand passive for the duration and take full responsibility for whatever is inflicted upon her.

The artist makes herself a statue on display. No longer made of skin and blood and sinew or containing thought or emotion. A mere object stripped of her humanness.

Someone approaches her with the jar of honey, putting the sweetness to her lips. Another chooses the red rose and places it delicately in the fingers of her left hand. A woman draws close to her to simply kiss her cheek as if giving thanks to a sacred statue. Someone offers her a drink of water from the bottle on the table.

Time stretches into hours; hours in which a certain innocence is shed and takes on a darker, menacing tone. Paint is used to write words on her chest and her arms. A scalpel cuts her neck and a stranger's lips suck the blood from the wound. The thorns of flowers are pressed into the soft flesh of her stomach.

Razor blades cut away the clothing from her body. Someone puts the single bullet into the chamber of the pistol and fits the gun in her hand, turning it inward to her own chest. Several have taken polaroid's throughout the performance, they place them in her hands like a Chinese fan on display to the audience.

For six hours the artist remains submissive and statuesque. The only visible signs of emotions are the silent tears that streak her face.

When the performance has come to an end and Marina once

again reveals herself as a woman and person among them, her audience is no longer able to face her. They turn away and leave quickly. Rather than confront the pain and violence they brought upon this woman they do not know, they do not look in her eyes. They do not speak. They simply run from her.

***

Rhythm 0 is a piece of living art that took place eight years prior to my birth but now cuts through to my core. I examine two side by side photographs taken during the performance. The first was taken two hours in: A fully clothed Marina stands, words written in red paint across her chest. Her face passive and unreadable. The second photo was taken six hours in: Her clothes removed. A streak of dried blood visible from her neck to her chest, becoming indiscernible from the red paint. Polaroids are held in her right hand. Tears on her pale cheeks. A woman violated. Robbed of dignity.

I look at photos and I watch interview clips with the artist discussing her experience of Rhythm 0. I feel anger. I feel disgust. I feel empathy. I want to step inside that room and wipe the tears from her face. I want to tell her how much I admire her bravery. I want to stop the ones who inflict the pain.

I wonder why when societal norms are removed from the equation and responsibility for one's actions lies outside the rules, the common denominator of human nature is violence?

I wonder at a person's ability to look beyond the humanity of another and to reduce that person to a mere object. What allows one to objectify and defile another's personhood?

I stand before a full-length mirror and try to imagine how it would feel to have strangers cut my clothes off my body. To feel hands touching my skin in too intimate a way. To feel the sting of scalpel cutting my flesh, my blood leaking from my body as if to prove that I am real. I imagine the weight of the pistol in my hand and the knowing that there is a very real bullet and that my life lies in the hands of these strangers.

I imagine the feeling of being violated. The physical violation of molestation and pain. The emotional violation of humiliation and degradation. Would I have been able to remain stoic as my body was fondled? Would I have been able to remain voiceless as I felt my skin being cut open?

I think of the tears on Marina's face and I wonder if she was appalled at the violence enacted on her body. Were her tears from the shock, that participants would be so willing to harm another person? Did she cry because it hurt her heart and her soul to see the ugliness humanity is capable of when given an opportunity?

Rhythm 0 was a performance intended as a social experiment of human nature. I would like to think that humanity is innately kind and good, more than carnal and demeaning but that is not what I see in the world I live in.

Cruelty in action and with words. Violence turned inward or onto another. Objectification. Injustice. Is that the meaning of human nature when all else is stripped away?

***

It is dusk. I stand on a wooden bridge watching the dark and colorless river flow beneath me. The trees lift their leafless branches to the gray sky as if petitioning the gods. The air is cool on my skin as day begins to pass over into night but I am restless and not yet wanting to retreat to home.

Movement below draws my attention and I turn my gaze to

the riverbank. A few hundred feet away I see three boys possibly eight or nine years of age. They each hold a stick-like object in their hands and they stand semi-circle around something round and solid on the ground between them. They are striking their sticks against the surface of this thing that I can't make out in the lengthening shadows. I am reminded of childhood birthday parties and candy-filled pinatas as I watch these boys determinedly try to break open whatever it is they have found near the river.

I make my way from the bridge down to the water's edge and walk slowly in the direction of the children. I am curious to see what has captured their attention.

As I draw closer I can see that the hard round object is the shell of a turtle. I see its motionless feet planted into the soft soil and its head retracted tight inside the safety of its shell. This poor creature is still alive, enduring quietly each blow of the sticks. Passive in the face of cruelty.

One of the boys has seen me. He drops his stick and motions for his friends to stop as I approach. Their faces resonate fear of reproachment then defiance then shame before the first to have seen me begins running in the opposite direction. The other two are quick to follow.

I am left alone with this scarred and changed animal, defenseless and motionless only fifty feet from the safety of the water. I stoop down and examine the extent of the damage inflicted. I can see the marks carved into the shell but it is not broken.

I think about Marina Abramovic after the six hours of Rhythm 0. The pain inflicted and endured as she maintained a passive and submissive demeanor. The people hurrying to be away from her when faced with the truth of their actions.

It is not so different from the children and this turtle. I wonder if this is humanity raw and bare when the threat of consequences is removed. If even the youngest among them can so easily view a living being as a mere object and in doing so are inclined towards pain and harm.

I reach out slowly to the turtle still hidden within its shell. I lift it carefully and bring it to the water's edge, putting it down in the shallows. I stand and wait and watch until tentatively it pokes its head into the open and furtively scrambles back to the safety of its watery home.

***

October 28th 2012. Vienna Austria.

Imagine a room with white walls. In this room are several tall and square and small tables, also white, arranged throughout the open space. In the center of each table a single squat and round candle flickering in the dimmed lighting. Wine glasses on every table reflecting the glow.

Imagine this room filled with people wearing white frocks over black clothing. They stand in groups of three or four, filling every table. Each individual is given a pair of white room silencing headphones. They are asked to wear these headphones for the next hour during the cocktail party. They are told they can make eye and physical contact during this time but they cannot speak.

There is an initial sense of awkwardness and discomfort as the hour begins. Some look around the room as if unsure what is expected of them. Some focus silently on the faces at their own table. As the participants ease into their time of silence they begin to move around the room. A simple gesture of a hand on another's arm. Some hug one another. Smiles are exchanged. One man stands stoically at his table observing the room but is clearly uninterested in interacting. A couple people at different points in the room stand reverently with eyes closed, seemingly at peace and enjoying the silence among a crowd.

Marina Abramovic moves through the room, sharing warm embraces and exchanging kisses on cheeks. This is her party. A performance art she titled The Silent Cocktail Party.

The hour comes to a close and headphones are removed. The room now fills with the sound of conversations and laughter as if a spell has been lifted.

The practice of silence among many as living art. Is it art because quiet and stillness is not the norm in a world in constant motion? Is it art because communication without words is not a natural behavior between strangers?

I like to think that when words are stripped away and body language and human touch replace the space of speech that one to another would be open and vulnerable. When words can no longer be used as expression how does that change the interactions of a group?

I think of the many ways language is used and I wonder if words dip below the surface to form the same connections among a people that wordless interactions do?

At one point during the hour of quiet Marina approaches a man standing alone with his eyes closed. His posture is relaxed and serene. Marina stands behind him, bows her head slightly and closes her eyes. They stand like this for a long moment and although there is no physical contact, there is an obvious connection that seems almost palpable between them. I wonder if the man senses her presence behind him, if he feels this shared moment that is occurring.

Sixty minutes of wordless communication. So much can be said without a single word spoken.

***

A large crowd has gathered in the park as I retrace my steps along my walk. Someone is handing out candles to each one gathered. The first is lit with a match and the flame held to the wick of the next candle and the next until all hold a glowing flame in their hands.

A posterboard sign near the entrance to the park explains why they are here. A candlelight vigil for suicide awareness. Beginning with a five minute interim of silence to honor the ones who have gone.

I join the group gathered, standing in the back in the darkening twilight. I am offered one of the candles and someone next to me holds out their own so I may light mine from their flame.

We remain silent as asked, the only sounds the shifting of bodies or the clearing of a throat. I hear some crying quietly and I watch them wipe their tears with tissues from their pockets. A woman touches the shoulder of the man weeping in front of her and I wonder if they know one another.

I feel the solemnity of the moment, the energy of grief and mourning that connects us in these minutes of quiet. I feel tears of empathy pool in my eyes and I don't try to wipe them away as they spill warm and salty over my cheeks.

The woman to my left who had lit my candle from her own holds out a tissue to me and when I accept it she gently squeezes my arm once in a kind gesture. I meet her eyes and see an expression of understanding, an entering into a shared moment with someone unknown. The moment passes in mere seconds but I feel as though something has been exchanged between us. That something has been shared that makes us less the strangers we were to one another minutes ago.

A thought runs through my mind as my eyes focus on the candle flame before me: This is the meaning of actions speaking louder than words.

***

I sleep deeply and dream in vivid images. I dream that I am within a building with four adjoining rooms, all of which have white walls and white tiled floors. I do not have a physical body, it is as if I am simply a presence in this empty space. The rooms are barren and hollow. I move between them as if searching for something within the emptiness.

There is too much white. Above me and below me and around me everything is painted white. When I am convinced that I am being swallowed up by the whiteness, I turn around and she is here, standing in the center as if she has always been here. She is dressed completely in black, a stark and shocking contrast against so much white space.

She cannot see me, I am only a presence here.

She holds a large tin pail that holds a dark red liquid and a wide bristle paintbrush. I watch as she moves past me to the farthest wall and sets the pail on the tiled floor. Her footsteps echo in the empty room.

She dips the brush into the wetness and swipes it with purpose on the white wall. The liquid is thin and runs in places. It is not paint. Somehow in my dream I am aware that she is painting in pigs blood. She is forming letters on the wall with the blood, letters that become a sentence: FRESH MORNING URINE SPRINKLE OVER NIGHTMARE DREAMS.

The blood is thin and pale and she traces over the letters until they are a deep dark color. She stands back to take in the full effect of her work. The lettering is vivid in the colorless room.

With pail and brush in hand she moves into the second white room. She contemplates the room for a moment before settling to begin again. Brush dipped into red blood. Blood on the white wall forming letters that form another sentence: SPIN AROUND UNTIL YOU LOSE CONSCIOUSNESS TRY TO EAT ALL THE QUESTIONS OF THE DAY.

I watch the color run slowly in streaks like tears of blood. I follow into the next room as she methodically dips and writes and traces: MIX FRESH BREAST MILK WITH FRESH SPERM MILK DRINK ON EARTHQUAKE NIGHTS.

The last room. The smell of animal blood lingering in the air. The final statement: WITH A SHARP KNIFE CUT DEEPLY INTO THE MIDDLE FINGER OF YOUR LEFT HAND EAT THE PAIN.

I stare at the words as they begin to dry. When I turn back to the room she is gone. I am alone. The tin pail of pigs blood and the paintbrush and her, all have gone as if I imagined it all happening. Her words on the walls of each room are the only trace of her having been here at all.

I draw closer to where a trickle of blood has run and I press my finger to its wetness. I bring my finger to my lips and taste of the blood with my tongue.

I awaken in the dark of my room. The taste of blood lingers in my mouth. I am still, feeling the movement of night air that seeps through my slightly open window. My eyes adjust to the darkness and I can see the familiarity of the wooden sculptures on their shelf, a linen scarf draped over the closet doorknob, the ceiling fan turning slow and silent above me.

I push back the blankets and in bare feet I make way by habit and moonlight to the kitchen. I prepare a cup of chamomile tea, letting it steep until the faintly nutty aroma fills my senses. Tea in hand I unlock the back door and enter the stillness of night to sit and sip and think.

I contemplate the details of my dream which came from a real occurrence in Italy in June 1997 that Marina Abramovic called Spirit Cooking. She referred to her painted scripts as "recipes".

I ponder these "recipes" and wonder if they are metaphorical with obscure meaning in the same way that a work of poetry might require interpretation. Or maybe simply the thoughts of an artist organized into a semblance of meaning understood by the artist alone.

The chill of the late night hour caresses me and I wrap my hands around the heat of my ceramic cup, drinking from its warmth. The stars are hidden behind veils of clouds but a sliver of pale moon hangs low above the treetops as if ensnared by their branches.

The meaning is in the blood, I think. Spirit Cooking as a work of art is demonstrative of the elements that make up humanity in their most basic sense. Pigs blood is the closest to blood of the human body. Breast milk. Sperm. Urine. Pain.

Organic ingredients that when mixed with flesh and muscle and bone are the unifying substances of our humanness. Broken down into raw and pure elements, are individuals really that different from one another?

***

By mid-morning a grayness has settled over the city and with it a damp fog that rolls in from the river.

I take the subway that will deposit me a block away from the arts district and the school where I have volunteered to pose nude for young art majors.

A dozen students sit with easels and supplies, observing the slope of my shoulders and the curve of my breasts and the soft flesh of my stomach, transposing my contours onto their canvases.

I try to make my body statuesque and my breathing shallow so as to be as still as possible. There is a feeling of vulnerability and sensuality in this moment. I feel exposed in an honest and real way that makes me feel more alive than I have felt before.

I think about the human body and the many forms it takes throughout one's lifetime. About the covetousness for youth and the innate fear of one's own mortality that most experience.

In 1995 Abramovic performed a series of installations called 'Cleaning the Mirror'. For the first installation she held an intact human skeleton on her lap. Beside her was a bucket of soapy water. Using a wooden scrubbing brush she cleansed the skeleton piece by piece. First the skull. Then the ribs. The hands. The pelvis. The feet.

Throughout this process the dust and filth was rinsed from the bones but began to coat the artists hands and her clothing as she worked. A transposing of death onto life as life cared for death. A blending together of life and death until one resembled the other. They are really not so separate as one will eventually become the other.

The second piece in the 'Cleaning the Mirror' series was of

the artist unclothed and lying on her back, knees bent, feet flat on the floor, arms at her sides. The skeleton laid on top of her, head on top of head, hands on top of hands, knees bent over knees, feet on top of feet. Bone on top of flesh. The artist drew oxygen into her lungs and exhaled it out. With each breath the bones of the skeleton rose and fell with her body. The effect is of life giving life unto death. Of life and death as shadows of one another. Life unable to escape its mortality.

I bring my focus back to my own body and the eyes that glance between it and their work and back again. I wonder if it has occurred to these students, as they replicate my shapes and lines, that each life is lived in the shadow of its death just as death shadows the living.

As they draw the curve of my hip or the vertebrae of my spine, I wonder if they realize that their art is a form of freezing time. The sketching of a body with graphite and charcoal and shadowed lines as a way of making permanent something that is temporal.

***

I imagine being in New York in 2002. Not to visit a place forever changed in the aftermath of a tragedy. Not to take in the sites or take pictures to become memories. I imagine being in New York in 2002 so I might visit the Sean Kelly Art Gallery and the original House with an Ocean View exhibition.

I imagine walking into the room at the gallery, white walls and gray cement floor. Three white platforms mounted on the back wall that resemble three small rooms without doors. Side by side with only an open doorframe to move from one to another. The first platform has a toilet and an open shower. The second a small wooden square table and a high-backed wooden chair. A metronome and a single glass of water upon the table. The last a long wooden bench that fills most of the length and mounted to the wall a wooden water fountain. Two wooden ladders are propped against the platforms but in place of rungs there are upturned butcher knifes.

I imagine seeing Abramovic sitting on the chair, her eyes closed and mind focused on the ticking of the metronome next to her. I imagine watching her in the stillness she emanates although crowds gather and disperse in the room. I wonder what will occupy her thoughts throughout the twelve days she will spend here without leaving these mounted rooms. For twelve days she will not eat and she will drink only the water from the fountain. She will use this toilet, this shower, this bench, this table and chair, this space, as her entire world for almost two full weeks.

I see myself sitting on the cement floor in front of this exhibition. The cold and the hard of it will not matter so absorbed in a deeper experience I will become. I imagine myself watching the artist lie on the bench/bed, looking out at the audience before her who gaze back. In my mind's eye I watch her rise and retrieve her glass to fill at the fountain, her movements slow and precise. When all that lies in the day ahead are hours to fill there is no reason for hurry.

I take in the simpleness of this life on display. Stripped down to the bare essentials needed for daily living it is obvious that lack of time is a delusion humanity has chosen by way of extraneous detail. I wonder about the things that occupy one's time in a day; the things that distract and overstimulate and numb and desensitize and leave one worn down at days end.

I think about those who have come to watch Abramovic as she sits sipping from her glass or taking a shower or resting on the bench. Most enter the gallery from curiosity and find themselves so absorbed that a few minutes turns into an hour or more and I wonder what it is that keeps them fascinated by the simple every day actions lived out before them. Is it longing for a simplified way of living that allows one to slow and enter fully into time? Is it a recognition that a culture has lost sight of what is truly important in a life?

I imagine in my mind the sound of the metronome in the quiet space of the three small rooms. I think the choice for silence and minimal comfort and the most basic of needs for such a period of time is about centering oneself, grounding oneself in a way that changes one's perspective. To connect with the inner self so that one may learn to connect with the world around them.

I sit in a quiet space and imagine taking away everything I think I need for comfort and the ways I fill the hours of a day. I imagine time spent without speaking or interactions, time without reading or music or television or distraction from self in any way. When my bodily functions and my thoughts are all I am left with, what would I learn about myself in a span of twelve days? What could I learn about time?

***

I walk past the harbor on my way back to the subway station. The docks are empty of boats; it's still too early for de-winterizing. The slate-colored water rolls and slaps around the sides, driven by a northerly sea breeze. A lone fisherman stands at the far end of the dock observing the waves that swallow his fishing line into the depths. He is still and patient and completely at ease. A person who is comfortable with himself and his place in the world and is unhurried by time.

I walk out onto the dock and stand far enough away so as not to intrude on his solitude. I take in the wide expanse of open sea that stretches beyond the harbor to where the water blends with the edge of the horizon. It is easy to believe that the edge is the end of the world. I close my eyes and fill my lungs with the saltwater air, exhaling slowly and quietly.

I hear the gravelly voice of the fisherman asking if there is a more peaceful place than this and I turn to him, unable to disagree. He sounds like the type who doesn't speak to others very often and instinctually I think he prefers it that way.

He is older in middle age I assume, with a kempt gray beard and well-worn cap and birkenstocks beneath his faded jeans. He tells me that he is passing through the area, that he couldn't pass up the opportunity to take in this scenery and drop a line in the water, that his home is that camper van parked in the lot behind us. He spends his days travelling to wherever the open road brings him, staying and leaving by no particular time frame.

I wonder for a moment how he makes his living but I do not ask. Instead I think about the freedom of such a simplistic life, the freedom to fill one's time however is desired. To spend the days absorbing what a life has to offer and focusing on the things that are needed to make a life. An inability to surround oneself with things because traveling requires less accessories and leaves room only for what is essential.

I watch the fisherman reel in his empty line and cast it out again with a practiced gesture that belies years of experience. I watch and I think in many ways this man has a fuller and richer life than most who strive for nothing less. A life lived deeper and wider in a way that most are always yearning for.

We share a comfortable silence, listening to the lolling water around us and I think again that there really is no place more peaceful than this.

***

I am still thinking about the fisherman as I ride the subway to my neighborhood and move with the crowd above to the sidewalk. Instead of walking toward home I head east in the direction of a brownstone I know well. A friend has invited me to a contemplative exercise she is teaching this afternoon and initially I had thought of not attending. Something about my brief interaction with the fisherman has changed my mind.

My friend greets me warmly with an embrace and peck on the cheek. I take a seat at the long polished wood table along with the six others waiting to begin.

In front of each of us there are two ceramic bowls. In one there is grains of white rice, the other black lentils. We are instructed to pour out the rice on the table in front of us. I do so, deliberately and slowly, so as not to scatter the grains over the table or onto the floor. I set the empty bowl back in its place on the table. Next, pour the lentils over the mound of rice, which I also do in the same careful and deliberate manner. Then, mix the two together.

I like the feel of the dry ingredients on my skin as my hands work them into a unified mass of black and white. I imagine it is the same meditative feeling one gets when kneading dough for bread or turning over warm soil for planting seeds.

When the rice and lentils are thoroughly mixed the exercise is simple: count the grains of rice. We are given a piece of paper and pencil to help tally as we go. We are to remain in silence as we complete this meditative practice as the intent is to demonstrate domination of the mind over the body.

It is relaxing and calming at first as I begin to arrange the rice in one pattern and the lentils in another. It is a natural inclination as time passes to become impatient when the black and white mound doesn't seem to be getting smaller as the body tenses and wants to move on to be doing something else. As more time passes the body feels discomfort in the neck and shoulders and back and wants the mind to be convinced that this exercise is throwing time away that could be spent in more productive ways. When one can resist the temptation to be rid of discomfort and the idea of time, the final stage is that of a relaxed mind and a peace found in the counting.

An exercise in will of the mind over will of the body. In not turning away from a thing that causes the body discomfort or pain. In not neglecting something that has begun once it becomes overwhelming or pointless or too difficult. Move forward. Move through. Keep counting.

My movements become methodical as my fingers move and separate and count. My mind wanders to a performance in Stockholm, Sweden that was in 2017. I meditate on this piece as a way of relaxing my body and my mind.

A hexagonal-shaped church. Set up outside the entrance is a white tent-like cloakroom that one enters before continuing in to the church. In this space one is required to leave coats, mobile phones, watches, cameras and bags. Shoes are removed. Nothing that may become a distraction is allowed to pass into the performance area inside.

Once inside the church there is a wide open sanctuary with high ceilings and hardwood floor. At certain intervals there are shapes outlined with tape across the flooring, some larger and wider and some smaller. Triangles and squares and X's.

There is the sound of singing echoing in the space, the

rhythmic soft sounds resounding off the walls and lifting to the vaulted space high above.

Abramovic is joined by thirty other performers who each slowly and consciously approach each one who enters and will escort one with slow and careful and measured steps to an area in the room.

Aside from the singers there is no noise. Silence is a requirement. Only bare feet on wood floor and the silent positioning of bodies is permitted.

As more and more enter the space the marked shapes on the floor become filled with strangers standing body to body. The X's are a place to lie down with heads at the center like petals of a human flower. Some stand alone in whatever space is available.

The performers guide each participant to their place and motion for eyes to be closed. They will circulate silently throughout the room, acting as a soothing support for the ones who have a powerful experience here.

Enter into stillness of the body. Stillness of the mind. The singing fills one's body with the sensation of fluidity. Stay in this space as long as one desires. Each individual is creating community among strangers through a shared experience.

Stillness of the mind. Stillness of the body. Keep counting.

***

It is the dark of night when I return home. Shrimp dipped in a cocktail sauce is dinner.

I wash my hands and splash water on my face. I look into the eyes of my mirror image, searching their depths for the secrets they hold.

If eyes are the windows to the soul, what is it that I reveal about my inner self to those around me when they look into my eyes? Did the woman at the candlelight vigil recognize the gentleness of a barefoot soul? Did the boys near the river see the depth of the well that is vulnerability? Did the fisherman at the harbor see trust as fragile as a papier mache sculpture?

What is trust? I do not believe in the definition of trust. I believe it's defined by each individual in many different ways and cannot be contained by one description no more than a single definition can describe love. It is felt and experienced in a myriad of ways and is not a constant.

1980. Marina Abramovic and her partner. A performance of trust.

She stands holding the handle of a bow. He stands opposite her holding an arrow taut against the bow string. They lean back slightly, their body weight creating the tension. An exercise of strength and trust. If one wavers and releases the tension the arrow will pierce her heart.

They face one another wordlessly, gazing at each other as they create this balance of equal trust.

I imagine the fatigued muscles of the arms and the cramping of the fingers as they hold the tension. There is an unflinching belief in the other that there will not be a letting go.

That is my belief about trust. That it is an arrow aimed at one's own heart and the responsibility lies within the self to choose wisely who the one standing opposite holding the string will be. The beauty lies in the truth that when the string is released and one is pierced by the arrow there is also the choice to move beyond the pain and to try again.

I lie between the coolness of my sheets and wait for the heat of my body to warm the space. I imagine myself holding the handle of a bow. Who is the one holding the arrow?

***

It is morning. I sit on my sofa holding the hand of a close friend. An hour ago he stood at my door, knocking, tears on his cheeks. The fighting in his home country has spread to his old neighborhood of Mariupol in Ukraine. Although he has spent his adult years here, his parents are still in Ukraine and now he has lost contact with them. I had opened my door to a face I didn't recognize. A face burdened with fear and concern and helplessness.

Now we sit in quiet together, watching the news coverage of a war so far away it seems surreal. Images of civilians protesting unarmed for their freedom while troops throw flash grenades and tear gas at the crowds. Black smoke filling the air from bombs that have decimated buildings and extinguished lives. More and more fleeing the pursuit of death with nowhere to go, but it is no longer safe to stay.

My friend leans forward toward the screen, elbows on knees but still holding my hand in his larger and warm one. His eyes are intense and I know that his mind can't help but wonder if his family lies buried beneath the crumbled debris that fill the streets or if they have been gunned down in an attempt to escape or even beaten and taken away as protestors joining a movement to fight for freedom.

I feel the same emotions now, of anguish and grief and injustice, that I experienced when I saw a white dress soaked in blood and a pile of bones that seemed like a mass grave.

A performance in Venice of 1997. Abramovic wears a white dress. She sits in the midst of fresh cow bones; piles of bloody bones as far as one can see. She is attempting to wash the bones one by one. In the process her dress turns from white to red and her hands and her feet become bloodstained. The water doesn't remove the blood from the bones and it can't take the red from her clothes. Her skin bears the evidence of blood that has been shed by the hands of others but now stains her own.

Piles of bones that represent piles of bodies. Lives taken by violence. Blood that seeped from war and stains all of humanity as none escape its effects. The stinking smell of death and decay and devastation.

I imagine soaking a soft washcloth in warm water and washing the calloused hands of my friend. Would the water wash away the stains of his hurt? If I gently cleansed his feet, would the water wash away the stains of his fear?

***

We wear layers to insulate us from the chilled wind. My friend and I walk toward the park, stopping at the stand of a coffee vendor before carrying our cardboard cups to a nearby bench.

He tells me stories of the Ukraine from his childhood. Of the Sultan Soleiman Mosque his family went to regularly. The paska his mother makes every Easter that he still misses. He describes her salo recipe in such detail I imagine I can taste the pork on my tongue. He wonders out loud if any of the places in his memories remain.

We are not alone in the park. I watch a couple teenage girls kick a soccer ball back and forth. A man walking his dog, the collar of his jacket upturned against the wind. A couple out for a walk, each holding a hand of the toddler between them. An old woman sitting on another bench tossing breadcrumbs to the pigeons around her feet.

It does not escape me the nonchalance of a people living out their ordinary lives, casually and without fear. There is no worry of artillery fire disrupting their time here in the park. No fear that homes have been demolished from a bomb strike. No need to seek refuge in another city or another country. No concern of seeing military tanks crowding the streets.

I wonder what creates this insulation of naivete. Has humanity become so accustomed to seeing wars and death and poverty played out on media outlets that all have become desensitized to the suffering?

A dichotomy of abandonment and control.

This concept was the focus of Rhythm 5 performed in 1974. A life-sized five point wooden star on the ground. The outline of the star is hollowed and filled with wooden shavings. The shavings are soaked with a flammable liquid. Marina Abramovic is there, dressed in black. She lights the wooden shavings. She walks around the outside of the flaming star and as she does so she cuts chunks from her hair and drops a handful into each point of the star. She then cuts her fingernails and walks around the outside of the star dropping the clippings into each point. She then cuts her toenails and walks a final time around the outside of the star dropping some into each point. Then Marina enters the star and lies down in its center. Eyes closed. Arms and legs spread out toward the points. She is completely surrounded by flames.

Is this what is necessary for re-sensitizing? To offer parts of ourselves as a homage to those who lost lives? To lie in the midst of the flames and feel the heat of the fire close and hot on one's skin to honor those who are suffering?

***

Imagine walking into an exhibition room at a gallery. The display is of a nude woman suspended on a blank wall, balanced on a bicycle seat. A white luminescent light is projected over her. She remains motionless, her body suspended in a way that makes her look like a three-dimensional work of art. Her eyes are open, unblinking, as she looks into the light that illumines her.

The effect is one of discomfort, pain, and strength of both body and mind.

After some time the effect becomes that of something on a deeper, more introspective level. A feeling of exposure and vulnerability. Aloneness. Transcendence of all of it.

It is Abramovic posed on the wall in her piece she called Luminosity, which was originally done in 1997.

I imagine the room filling and emptying and filling again with those who are curious onlookers, some who are followers of the artist and some who are note taking for their columns. Amidst the flow of moving bodies there is one, unmoving and silent, who remains painstakingly visible. One among a room of many but very much alone.

I wonder if the feeling of aloneness is the same as loneliness? Does one's feelings of exposure and pain make the loneliness greater than the aloneness? Or is it reversed? Is it either?

At what point does the mind move past noticing the pain of the body and arrive at the knowing that beyond the pain, beyond the difficulty, beyond the aloneness, beyond the nakedness and the fragility of the moment, that the spirit is unbreakable?

That is what I am thinking of now, as I sit on this park bench sipping from a paper cup. I wonder if my friend has the same feelings of aloneness and fragility being among so many who don't understand war as personal? There is pain and vulnerability in the not knowing if loved ones are safe or even living. There is pain and vulnerability in seeing the devastation of a country and people he loves.

I wonder if it is through the pain and vulnerability and difficulty that the strength of spirit becomes illumined.

***

The weight of war and grief remains like an ink blot on paper when I am alone. There is a need for peace and solitude rising within me that is not unlike the craving for a drug.

I follow a well-worn trail in the woods, the whispering of the trees and my footsteps on last year's autumn leaves replacing the noise of city traffic and human voices. The song of a bird. The fleeting sound of little squirrel feet scampering nearby.

I am surrounded by black birch, sugar maple, sturdy pine. I listen to their hushed voices so delicate in my ears and I think of their unseen interconnectedness. That below the dark soil their thick roots spread toward one another. That there is a sharing of nutrients and carbon dioxide among them if one has surplus and another is in need. That they protect one another by sending signals of warning to others if one becomes infected with parasite.

There is wisdom and peace to be found here. I settle at the base of a black birch and lean against its sturdiness. I close my eyes and breathe deep of the purity that is nature. I understand the sense of connectedness that lies between Mother Earth and human nature and the sense of beauty and power that lies within both.

I imagine it was something close to this that Marina felt when she stood naked in the mouth of a cavernous opening in Brazil. The picture speaks to the incredible power and beauty of

Mother Earth but there is also a gentleness in the way the mouth of the cave surrounds the naked human body like holding one within its womb. An attestation of something profound and spiritual and moving.

There is a feeling of internal calm and submission to something greater than humanity that lies outside oneself as I let myself relax into the bark of the tree that holds me. I imagine this is the same feeling of peace and surrender one feels entering into a great cathedral.

With eyes closed I breathe deep this feeling that is so similar to something spiritual. I imagine myself with roots that reach out around me to draw from the natural strength and energy found here.

I exhale.

***

In 1996 Abramovic did a video performance of herself eating a large raw white onion. The frame is of her long dark hair loose around her shoulders and her face, pale against her red-painted lips. Her eyes are focused on something above and unseen and she holds up an unpeeled onion with red-painted fingernails.

She bites into the onion as one would a sweet apple, her eyes upturned and focused. She eats of the rawness, chewing and swallowing methodically. She bites deeper towards its center, its outer layers flaking into her palm and leaving traces of onion around her mouth and on her chin. Her actions become more voracious as her teeth tear deeper into the flesh. The red on her lips begins to smear around her mouth. The bitterness on her tongue causes saliva to run over her chin. Tears course down her cheeks to blend with the saliva and bits of onion near her mouth.

She blinks through the stinging of her tears, her gaze never wavering from her focus above. Her expression is one of burden and weariness as if she is beseeching the gods.

I think of the many layers of an onion as the many layers of a self. The skin is thin and fragile and falls away easily like a protective facade. The outside layer is smooth and firm and offers the first taste of bitterness on the tongue as if an offering of more to be discovered. Beneath that is an awakening of the senses as a preparation for what is to come. As one moves through the layers of the middle there is a deeper intensity of what has been revealed. The center is the smallest and rawest part of a self where the flavor begins and emanates out from but the most rarely revealed.

At the end of the performance a messy outer layer of onion is all that remains. A representation of the messiness of a life. The smeared red lips and the tear-filled eyes like the imperfections that mark all of humanity.

Her fingers with their red nails still clutching what is left. An unwillingness to let go even when the layers are peeled back and the rawness and bitterness of a life have been swallowed down.

***

It is this feeling of rawness I keep with me as I walk toward home. I want to know what is hidden beneath the layers of a self. I think about the complexity of an individual and wonder if one can ever really know the foundation upon which the self was formed. What traumas, what challenges, what heartaches have been borne to become the self as one is now?

Does one rise out of the ashes of another's history? Does one carry forward familial traumas and tragedies from a life lived before one came into being? Are the layers of a self-sculpted by imprinted emotions from the time of birth?

I wonder if one creates a self throughout a lifetime or if the self-forms it's layers from the raw materials of memories and experiences and emotions of a life.

I stand before the mirror and consider my reflection until the shape of my eyes and the structure of my nose and the curve of my lips blur and I become a reflected mass of a face. I contemplate what is beneath the layer of my flesh and beyond the rushing blood in my veins and beyond the drum of my heart; what lies inside my deepest layer of self that has yet to be discovered and brought forth.

Is that the meaning of a life, a continuation of searching and discovering? Isn't that what art reflects, the new layers of a self that have been peeled away and are shared with the rest of humanity to learn from and to grow with?

I find my camera tucked away on a closet shelf and return to the mirror. I photograph an eye up close, my color vivid and pupil direct. A hand with fingers spread. The curve of one leg. An ear. My mouth. My nose. A breast. I photograph the pieces that make up an exterior and I print them out.

I form a collage of my photographed body parts and I take a knife to pierce the skin of my palm and I use the blood of my body to paint over the collage. A representation of the parts that make a whole. Of the flesh and blood that hold the pain and the history and the memories.

***

There is a place in Kyiv Ukraine where a 131 foot long wall, constructed of anthracite from Ukrainian mines and rose quartz crystals from Brazil, was unveiled in October of 2021 as another installation of Marina's work. This 'Crystal Crying Wall' is symbolic of Jerusalem's 'Wailing Wall' and was erected as a physical remembrance and honoring of the largest massacre of Jewish people that occurred during World War Two.

Although the 'Crystal Crying Wall' came into being for the 80th anniversary of the deaths of so many, this artwork is representative of the lives taken in any war and is a place for remembering and for healing.

I imagine a slow and contemplative walk along the wall, bare feet in the dirt so I may fully experience this place and let it leave traces of itself behind on my skin. I imagine fingertips feeling the dark and solid anthracite, tracing each uneven surface and crevice. A feeling of grief and respect and of spirit transposed here from all the ones who have come to remember.

I imagine the rose quartz stuck into the rock, an offering of strength and healing. I see myself leaning in until forehead rests on the crystal, hands firm on the wall and eyes closed. A moment of silence and of acknowledgment and a transferring of energy.

I feel the importance of this place as I remember that humanity carries with it the weight of familial history, of geographical history, of wars and death and blood that stain the earth. Here is a place to honor a shared history, to remember the violence that altered a people and to find some solace in.

***

I sit in a darkened auditorium not far from the raised staging where the musicians sit cross-legged on the floor. Elaborate carved wooden drums and tin pieces on wooden frames. A soft staging light that illumines the group. From the silence begins a soft rhythmic sound of a wooden instrument on tin, a peaceful soothing rhythm. The sound of the musicians' palms tapping the hide of the wooden drums joins the rhythm of the tin. Wooden flutes join in the sound and the room fills with the gentle music.

My counting-the-grains-of-rice friend has accompanied me to this gamelan drumming performance and she sits next to me as we are both caught up in a movement of graceful sound. I close my eyes and feel the rhythm with my senses, allowing the music to evoke a feeling of warmth and peace that fills my being.

In my mind I visualize a photo I love of Abramovic taken during a trip to Brazil. She sits in a wooden chair facing away from the photographer in the center of a desert canyon that has been eroded by monsoons and windstorms and the creativity of Mother Nature. Sandstone walls rise around her, the rock carved by natural forces.

The photo is beautiful in its simplicity. A barren and challenging landscape in which somehow life manages to survive. Healthy green scrub brush populate the canyon floor, somehow rooted in the desert soil and persisting through the harsh elements.

There is a feeling of meditative calm and a centering of oneself in a place so beautiful yet so deceiving. It belies the possibility of healing for one's spirit and a peace for the mind.

I hold onto this centering calm as the music fades and the room is quieted. I remain in meditative stillness as the room empties of the crowd, incorporating the sounds and sensations into the fabric of my body like a new layer of sensory memory. I can sense in her stillness that my friend has had a similar experience in this place. Her head is bowed and palms held together over her face as if a monk in meditative prayer.

Beauty found within simplicity.

***

Evening has settled in around us, whispering its secrets to the wind. My friend and I sit on my deck, sharing a bottle of red and a carefully rolled joint. The tartness of the wine settles on my tongue and I like the way the air caresses my skin. I look to the sky as my friend holds the joint to her lips with delicate fingers, but there are no stars or moon above us. The sky is a darkening blank canvas.

Our voices are lifted in the winds and tossed to the atmosphere as our conversation centers on the hatred and division and chaos and violence of a world that has forgotten how to feel peace and empathy. There is a need for discovery of purpose and of self and of awareness. A need for cultivating love of self and of spirit so that one may learn to put that energy back into a world so desperate for healing.

I accept the joint passed to me and inhale of its earthiness as my friend speaks of a world that does not know how to slow and appreciate and contemplate. There is too much hurrying through the days and too little reflection. There is no time for silence and stillness and centering and one no longer recognizes the internal yearning that persists for silence and stillness and centering in the midst of the chaos.

I remember an image framed and hung on a white wall space within the room of a gallery. The image focuses on Abramovic sitting in the center, her black hair pulled back and her body clothed in black. She sits in a darkened place with eyes closed serenely and in her left hand she holds a lit white candlestick. The glow of the flame softly illumines her face and creates an aura of light around her that dispels the darkness. The photo is part of a series she called 'With Eyes Closed I See Happiness'.

I drink of the wine like one taking communion; a sacred offering to be savored with meaning. I tell my friend about the photo in the museum and reflect on how different of a world we would experience if humanity had learned how to seek happiness from within instead of in the shallowness of things external. A constant seeking and grasping for a temporary illusion of happiness but always fading like a dream in the light of morning.

I imagine that if one grasps the meaning of happiness found within the self, only then can one understand the feeling of sitting in stillness and darkness and with eyes closed see happiness illuminating like the glow of a candle flame in the dark.

***

Maybe it's the wine or maybe it's the weed or a combination of both, but this night I dream of darkness and flames. I don't recognize this place but I know I have been here before. I am outside and I am naked and I am cold. I am cold because it is snowing, large white flakes floating in the air like crystallized confetti. The flakes fall thick and fast but nothing is coating the ground. I see the orange glow of flames through the veil of snow and I walk toward it. It is night and darkness is everywhere. There is only the white of the snow falling and the beckoning of the fire. A circle of stones and within the circle the flames. I look away from the fire and suddenly there are men and women, naked as I am, all seated around the circle of fire. They sit in shared silence and as I glance at their faces I see that the eyes of each one have been burned away. In place of eyes there are flat stones. A woman with eyes the color of clouds lit by sun steps barefoot from the flames. She approaches me with slow steps as if conscientious of her movements. She stands in front of me, too close, and takes both my hands in her own. A confident smile plays on her lips as she tells me that now is the time for my purification so that I may be like the others. A slow comprehension settles in me and I understand that she means to take me into the fire. I resist her grasp of my hands but she won't let me go. She holds tighter like I am a disobedient child and the smile falls away from her lips. The snow is falling so thickly I can't see anything in the darkness and she is stronger than I am. She pulls me closer and closer to the fire and I can feel the heat of the flames on my naked skin and I am afraid. She whispers close in my ear that I need to be purified and that this is the only way. She pushes me into the fire and I am falling...

I awaken in the safety of my bed. I can smell the smoke from the fire lingering in my hair and my ears are full of the sound of the crackling flames. I breathe deeply. I am alive.

***

Imagine standing outside a gallery where an attendant places a blindfold over the eyes and noise cancelling headphones over the ears before being led inside. All personal effects have been taken away so there is pure experience without distraction. The gallery is void of everything except for the sensory deprived bodies around the rooms. The participants have become the performance. There becomes a hyper-awareness of the body in relation to this space and in relation to those who share the space.

This participant as performance setting occurred in 2014 at MoMA in New York City. Abramovic was present at random times throughout the six days the event took place, so those who entered the sensory deprivation gallery were not aware if one was interacting with the artist herself or if she was even present at all.

The performance was designed for one to enter an environment where time itself slows its pace. There is a slowing of the body and its movement. A slowing of the mind and the thoughts that clutter and race.

With all sound and external visual stripped away there is simply a turning inward to oneself. A time for internal reflection and connection with the self. A focus on the energy one gives to the space around itself and feeling the energy of the others filling this space. A learning how to be completely present in one's self and completely aware of those sharing the same space in the same time.

I imagine the peace that settles into one's spirit once the body is accustomed to not seeing and not hearing. A feeling of reconnecting with time and self. A learning to slow and savor the experience of just being without demand and expectation and stimulation.

I think about the ones who spent hours inside the gallery and I wonder if there was a sensory shock when they stepped outside into the crowded and noisy and rushing city streets. I wonder if there was a recognition of too much stimulation in a world that has become too hectic. If there was a new awareness of how to slow and stretch the time given in a day so that there may be more experiencing the world and less rushing through it.

I imagine a conscientious way of living through a day that allows one to stay connected to oneself. I wonder if living in full awareness would change the interactions of people with each other and with the environment that becomes the shared space. A learning to live beyond sight and hearing, to experience one another and the world with all senses.

***

There is a cement wall that encloses a children's playground near the city's park. A structure of imposed safety wherein littles can run and play and be the children they are without worry of one dashing into the flow of traffic or wandering beyond the safety of the play area.

This cement wall has been defaced with the graffiti of those who disrespect the innocence of children. A colorful display of slang words and sexually explicit images now cover the length of the wall. Words that imply a sense of masochism and female inferiority, of domination and objectification. Images representative of a culture that has effectively desensitized and manipulated the way a body is viewed and treated.

A group of volunteers from the youth center have joined at this place with buckets of paint and supplies to erase the debasement that occurred in the cover of night.

I approach one of the volunteers and am warmly received to help in making this a welcoming place once more. With a bucket of white paint and brush I begin to coat over the dirty words spray painted with yellow and black and blue. The colors of a bruise.

I think about the words that are spoken in daily casual conversations that segregate and isolate and divide and I wonder if there is a comprehension about the way words are used. Is there an understanding of the power of speech and the effects that words can have? Does one realize the impact of something that once put out into the open cannot be retracted or erased? I think about the energy spent in teaching the youngest generation about what is and isn't a kind thing to say but I realize the lack of accountability among the adults. I wonder if one realizes the sense of hypocrisy that is unknowingly being imprinted onto the most impressionable who see the actions of others and learn to mimic speech.

I spread the white paint evenly in broad strokes over the cement wall and I imagine being able to coat over the ugliness of humanity, to create a place where the ones to come can make something beautiful in its place.

***

Wine. Honey. Razor blade. Whip. Block of ice. Military cap and boots. Wooden staff. The implements used for Abramovic's original performance of The Lips of Thomas in 1975.

The artist stood nude amidst an encircling crowd and with the edge of the razor blade she made a cut in the flesh of her stomach, the first point of a five point star. With a white cloth she blot the blood that slowly seeped up and out of her skin and then slipped her feet into the boots. She placed the military hat on her head and held the wooden staff, tears running from her eyes as a Russian folk song played. Then, with composure, off with the boots and the hat and she moved to the blocks of ice that formed a cross shape. She laid on the ice until her body was cold and shivering. Then she took the whip and knelt on the floor, lashing her chilled skin over and over. Then she moved to the table that held the honey and the wine. She ate of the honey. Drank of the red wine. Then she repeated the process over and over in succession: Cut into the stomach, put on the military hat and boots and pick up the staff, lie on the ice, whip the bare cold flesh, eat of the honey and drink of the wine. For hours the sequence repeats until, at the end, Abramovic kneels naked on the floor, her stomach cut and bleeding, the skin of her back red and welted, her face wet with tears and her eyes consumed with a deep sorrow.

Although the original performance attests to repression of both a communist culture and an orthodox religion the two ideas are symbolic of a new time in the world. I contemplate the cross-shaped ice, the self-flagellation, the honey and the wine as the physical components imposed by organized religion and the constraints of the mind and body that are taught. I want to believe there is more to spirituality than religion. I think about the rules and regulated rituals inherent in a religious practice and I wonder where the freedom is.

I think about the military hat and boots and the cutting of the star into the skin and I compare it to a society that gives power to the already powerful and wealth to the ones already wealthy. A mainstream sense of greed and hunger that is fostered while a majority live as self-sacrificial lambs shedding their own blood in an effort of pure existence.

***

I step into the hot bath and sink slowly into its warmth, steam rising and breathing onto the mirrors of the bathroom. I lie on the bottom and let my hair fan around me in the lapping water. There is the scent of jasmine essential oils that waft in the air and soak into my skin. I close my eyes and sink beneath the surface, my ears filling with the movement of water and my body weightless and fluid. I am still, the water ceasing over me as if in a watery grave that has claimed me and holds me. An embryo within its amniotic fluid, safe and warm and protected.

I wonder at the strength and resiliency of the body and its tolerance for pain and torture and damage; its ability to heal and create life. I think about the standards and projections that are imposed on the body and the importance of it in the eyes of others. There are judgments and assumptions and expectations but I wonder where one learns this pattern of thinking. I wonder if there is one cause or if the root of it all encompasses many sources like an ocean being fed from multiple waterways. An infection of the mind of people like a water source that has been polluted.

I open my eyes from below the water and look up at the wavering and blurry clouds through the skylight above me. I like this feeling of buoyancy and disconnect from gravity like I can leave this world for even a short time.

I think about Marina from her 1975 performance at an art festival in Copenhagen she titled 'Art is Beautiful, The Artist Must be Beautiful'. A simple one-hour performance in which she stood topless before a camera with her long hair loose around her face. In one hand she held a metal comb and in the other a metal brush. She begins to brush her hair in a slow and methodical manner while repeating out loud "Art is beautiful, the artist must be beautiful". As the performance progresses her movements become more fervent and aggressive as she combs and brushes her hair again and again. She continues to repeat over and over "art is beautiful, the artist must be beautiful", her voice becoming more strained and aggressive. Her face belies the pain and strain as the more she combs and brushes the more damage she does to her scalp and hair and face.

I rise above the surface and let my lungs take in oxygen. How does one define what is beautiful and why does beauty matter?

***

To breathe in is an intake of oxygen. To breathe out gives carbon dioxide. A symbiotic relationship of taking in life and giving life into the environment. A give and take. Not unlike relationships of human nature in which a codependency of one to fulfill the needs of the other exists in a basic physical and psychological way. In a love relationship it is this that allows one to sustain the other. It is a delicate balance that can become imbalanced when there is more taking than giving in a relationship. It is as if one has taken a candle and enclosed it within a case of glass; the oxygen dwindles and the flame slowly loses life and flickers out. If there is only a taking and the symbiosis no longer exists how can one sustain?

In 1977 a beautiful demonstration of this imbalance was performed in Belgrade by Abramovic and her partner. Surrounded by an audience while filming the performance, the artists knelt facing one another. With cigarette filters in their nostrils and their mouths pressed together as if in a lovers kiss one breathed into the other and the other would take of the exhalation and then breathe in return to the other. A back and forth of give and take. Except the oxygen passed into one became carbon dioxide passed to the other and back again. The oxygen supply became extinguished and the artists had to stop when coming close to losing consciousness from lack of oxygen.

Watching the performance is like an illusion of two people wholly consumed in one another and one doesn't realize as a spectator that they are slowly taking life from each other. A candle enclosed within a glass case.

Balance. Equanimity. Equality. The components that give oxygen and life to sustain relationship.

***

The smell of fresh cut wood lingers in the air, reminiscent of the smell of my father's workshop at my childhood home. Wood shavings carpet the floor around the work space in the multi-ethnic novelty shop where I am browsing. I watch the Indonesian wood carver as he expertly works the soft limewood with a chisel, his face expressionless yet somehow serene as he works. With the basic shape carved out he replaces the chisel with a wide skew to start the detailing, his movements precise and practiced. A smaller skew for smaller detail and finally a veiner for the smallest definition.

I watch as a simple block of light wood in the skilled hands of this artist has now become a wooden idol of Buddha. A beautiful icon from the raw material of nature transformed.

The wood carver carefully sands the Buddha smooth and examines it for any imperfections. I am surprised when he holds it out to me and nods encouragingly for me to take it. I hold the palm sized icon and admire out loud his handiwork. The wood carver bows his head in gratitude and tells me he would like me to have it, shaking his head definitively when I ask him how much to pay for it.

The wooden Buddha sits contemplatively in a cross-legged position with carved arms in prayer position and closed eyes. I imagine the Indonesian wood carver saying his prayers to an icon like this one in his home; maybe even as part of a sacred shrine. Not unlike those who have statues of Jesus or wear a cross around their neck. I contemplate the act of prayer and the sacrosanct emotion imposed on objects like the small Buddha I hold in my hands.

I wonder if having something tangible to hold on to and to see with the eyes help those to believe in something that is unseen. Maybe it is not enough to sit within the walls of a church and listen to the lessons of a Book for some to feel connected to their God. Maybe it is not enough for some to meditate and practice the eight-fold path to feel spiritual enlightenment.

I have memories of being told 'seeing is believing' and I imagine it must be the same for those seeking spirituality in a world gone mad. To see something that resembles goodness and hope and belief that there is something more that is beyond here when 'here' is a place that is hard and existential and painful.

The wooden Buddha I place on my bedroom shelf, in the center of the wooden statues. I like to think that I can feel the peace and calm that it represents filling this space.

***

Mid-afternoon of the first real warmth of spring. The sun is warm on skin and for the first time in months layers are not necessary to protect against the chill.

I walk the city streets with camera in hand, wanting to capture photos of the things that make me feel peace. I photograph the old stone Pentecostal Church with its beautiful stained-glass windows glowing in the light. I photograph the way the sun shines through the branches overhead, enhancing the new-grown leaves that are just beginning to bud. I photograph a young mother nursing her newborn and the shared bond exchanged in this nurturing act. An elderly couple kissing on the sidewalk like still-young lovers. I capture a bouquet of sunflowers outside a flower shop within my frame and photograph their essence of beauty. A mural of artwork on the side of a brick building. Children's hands held together.

Simple and normal things that remind me of the beauty

found in the ordinary. That peace and goodness and innocence still exist in a place where darkness seems to overtake the light. In the midst of a culture in love with self and materialism and commercialism and consumerism there still exists the raw materials of a life waiting to be found and savored. A peace and happiness that cannot be bought, it can only be discovered.

I like to think that this was the basis for Abramovic's healing method of advising her audience to find a tree that one felt a connection to; not based on the beauty of it but on a felt sentimentality. Inspired by the dances of Indigenous people around the sequoia trees Abramovic recognized the peace and healing to be found in the ordinary and advised her public to feel the texture of the bark, to hug their tree and know that it is a living thing that interacts with its environment.

Peace found in the ordinary. So I photograph the movement of the river from atop the wooden bridge where I had seen the boys and the turtle. I take a picture of an older man reading his book in the park. A flock of geese flying in formation.

I point and click and savor the simple and normal things that wait to be discovered.

***

I sit on the chaise in the solitude of my apartment, a plate of chicken salad on Ritz is dinner. I watch a televised interview with a gender and sexuality studies professor discussing pronoun acknowledgement and the importance of removing gender and identity barriers in society. The ways in which misgendering can effect one's mental wellbeing and sense of self in the world. To examine the ways by which gender is defined and why.

I think about the many ways one may feel uncomfortable in

a body or in a name that assimilates to a person one doesn't feel they identify as. I wonder what can be seen as offensive in a being who only wants the freedom to create the person they are. Isn't that how we define individuality and self-expression? I think about gender barriers and why they exist in the first place. I wonder who gets to decide what is right and what is wrong for another to do what is right for themself? How does one define man or woman and why does it have to be either/or? I want to know where the idea that humanity is linked by simply being human fell by the wayside and who are the ones to benefit from division and discrimination?

It was in Italy 1977 that Abramovic and her partner performed Imponderability, an art piece that forced the audience to face their assumptions about gender in a very close and discomforting way. The two artists stood nude facing each other in the doorway of an art gallery, posing as "living doors." This positioning forced the ones entering the gallery to squeeze sideways between the naked bodies, and in doing so, to choose spontaneously which body to turn toward upon entrance. The point was to have no forethought about why one chose to turn toward the male artist or the female artist. The spontaneity of choice didn't leave time for the one pushing through to think about why. One walked past the "living doorway" on internal assumptions about their own identity and gender. The performance was abruptly ended by police after 350 people had already passed through.

Imponderability was re-performed at MoMA in 2010 by four performance artists who switched up the original by posing two women as the doorway or two men and sometimes one of each. Some audience members were so uncomfortable they chose to walk around and avoid the doorway altogether.

I think about the new technology that now enables new parents to choose the gender of their baby instead of genetics making that choice for them, and I think about those who want to choose their own gender as they discover themselves. I want to know, is there a difference between them?

***

The morning is cloudy but warm, a fine mist falling like a spritz of fragrance from the heavens. The weather has not deterred the crowd gathered in the city square for today's march for peace to support Ukraine. I find my East Slav friend in front of the water fountain as planned. I have come to show my support for him and for the innocent in a country torn apart by violence.

Blue and yellow flags sway in the air and almost everyone here carries a homemade sign or banner of support. We move as one down the street. My friend begins to sing the national anthem of his country of birth, "Ukraine has not yet perished." He sings the words in his native language so I am only able to recognize a few. Other native Ukrainians hear his singing and join in, banners held high as we walk the city blocks.

There is a feeling here of unity and solidarity for a shared purpose. It is true that there is strength in numbers, I can feel the charge of energy amongst us. There is a lightness about my friend that wasn't present the morning he came to my apartment and we watched the devastation of war on my television. He tells me that he has had contact with his father and that both his parents are alive and okay. They have made it safely to Wroclaw in Poland after being delayed at the border for several days. A kind Polish family volunteered to house them like so many families have done in the first days of war. I am glad for him and for them and the obvious relief that is etched in the lines of his face.

I take his hand as we walk and it doesn't escape me the willingness of many to come together to show unity when there is tragedy of a large scale. It is during times of conflict such as terrorism, wars, political trials and racial strife that humanity will join together and raise their voices. It is then that they will demonstrate and protest and write letters to their legislation and form social media groups to rally an alliance.

I can't help but wonder where the alliance and the rallying cries and the show of unity reside to end the poverty of those working for pennies on the dollar to feed large families. To end the hunger that not only continues in other countries but also here where it is common to think it's not an issue and a large population turn a blind eye to the need. To end the prejudice and discrimination and hatred that cause division.

I think about the sharing of resources to fund science and medicine and political campaigns and wonder what impact could be made if there might be a global sharing of resources. Who would be in need if there was a unity of sharing surplus?

I feel my friend squeeze my hand and the gesture brings me back to this present moment. We make eye contact and smile and he raises the blue and yellow flag in the air. This march for peace has an impact for him and his family. Being here, being a part of this for him and with him; this is a beginning.

***

Imagine a quiet solitary moment engulfed by Mother Nature. Stand barefoot on the soft and moist soil, rooted to this organic place. Hear the songs of the birds within the tree branches and the air moving the leaves above and below. See the sun reflecting on the ground, illuminating the decay of old leaves and dropped pine needles, and the thick textured bark of the trees that surround. Smell the earthy aroma of being in nature. Feel the calm and the stillness that invite one to linger here.

Imagine that there is a hand mirror and with this mirror one is to hold it up in front of the face and look at the reflection of the place where one stands.

Imagine exploring this place through the mirror walking backward for four hours.

This is an exercise Abramovic created to help with her art performance work and has now become an adopted practice among many, a part of The Abramovic Method.

When reality is a reflection and we are conscientiously moving through it how does one's perception of it change?

I wonder if there becomes an awareness of something new and commonly overlooked in the constant motion of moving forward and looking ahead instead of looking around. If what is reflected back offers a clarity that is otherwise obscured. If changing the focus of how one views and thinks of the space inhabited also changes the focus of the mind. Does it make one's thoughts more reflective and conscientious in the way that it does the body?

The mind and body share a relationship of connection that can also function independently of one another. Abramovic demonstrated this in 1974 as a piece she titled Rhythm 2. For the first part of her performance she swallowed a pill that is prescribed for catatonia. The medication is meant to keep one's muscles in movement when there is none. The effect for Abramovic was one of uncontrolled body movement and seizures. The artist experienced complete lack of control over her body but her mind was clear and very aware of what was happening.

The second part of the performance occurred ten minutes after she fully recovered from the effects of the pill. For this, Abramovic swallowed a second pill normally taken for aggressive behavior or depression. The effect was the opposite of the first; the artist's body was physically present but her mind was elusive and she described the feeling as if her mind was not fully there. She had no memory of this part of the performance when the drug had worn off and had not been aware of what her body was doing.

Rhythm 2 was meant as an exploration of the mind-body connection and I wonder if it is that feeling of disconnect from one's body or one's mind that so many seek when illegal drugs are pumped into the body. An escape from a reality that is too hard to face and an artificial feeling that invokes the wanting of more. A sacrifice of mind and body for a reality of one's making that remains obscured until a mirror is held up to reflect back what has been hidden.

I want to lower the mirror and close my eyes. I want to feel my way through with sharpened senses. I want to feel fully alive.

***

I have the prints of the photographs taken of the simple and ordinary things along my walk. I trim and cut and paste and create a collage of these peaceful images. I cut newspaper headlines of murder and robbery and kidnapping and shootings and modge podge them over the photos of peace until the words are so faded they are hardly there at all. The photos beneath show through the papers transparency; a triumph of good over evil. The final piece is a photo of Marina I paste in the center of it all.

The photo is of the artist lying flat on a narrow cot. Eyes closed as if in sleep or a meditative state. Beneath the cot is a row of white candlesticks all lit with white glowing flame. A still life of peace and the embodiment of mind body and spirit in connection.

I place the finished collage next to the first of body images painted over with blood.

***

A taxi takes me to the outskirts of the city where land is interrupted by the sea. The taillights fade into the dusk and I am alone. I follow a footpath that brings me down to a rocky shore. The area is vacant and secluded and the only sound is the rushing of the waves toward the shoreline. I slip off shoes and socks and walk the length, small sharp stones biting my sensitive soles so I walk slowly, conscientiously, aware of every step.

Where beach abuts with dunes I stand and linger, gaze surveying the wide open expanse of water before me. I make my way back to where I left my shoes, stepping around seaweed and driftwood brought in by the shifting tides.

Dusk deepens to the darkness of early night. The emptiness and seclusion and cover of dark embolden me to remove my clothing and wade into the sharp cold of the waves. My skin stings and resists and I am breathless but I dive to the bottom and swim out until the shore behind me seems nothing more than a shadow. The sense of vulnerability and the smallness of my existence in a vast space is sharpened in a way one doesn't realize when used to city buildings and crowded streets.

I feel my body becoming numb and heavy from the startling temperature and I swim to shallow water, making my way back onto the beach and dry clothes.

I wander the shore, gathering larger rocks into a pile until I have enough. I make a circle from the rocks, remembering the circle of fire from my dream, and then I sit on the sand in the middle of the circle. I have a winter coat, a knit hat and my gloves for what little warmth I can keep close to my body. I have brought nothing else, nothing to eat or drink or phone to distract. I have come here to fast and to test the will of body and mind when feeling deprivation and discomfort.

I watch the movement of the sea beneath the dark sky, the glinting of moonlight on water the only thing to separate one from the other. I think about the many connections between a human body and the earth that sustains it. How the rings of a tree so closely represent the rings of a thumbprint. How the branching veins in a body are not unlike the spreading roots of a tree. How the lines of a human palm are so similar to the lines of a fallen leaf. The way a human lung looks the same as the view of spreading branches when lying beneath a tree and looking to the sky.

I contemplate the interconnectedness of life and the amnesia of this awareness. I breathe it into my lungs and I feel the damp sand where I sit. I am still and silent in the dark. I wait for the dawn.

***

The first sign of light is creeping into the sky when I leave my sanctuary of the beach. The world is still asleep and quiet. The birds are beginning to wake in an early search for food. An occasional light in a window as I pass by makes me think of night-filled dreams giving way to the putting on of slippers and the scent of coffee brewing in kitchens.

The dampness of the beach sand and the cold of night have sunk into my bones and I feel the stiffness of joints and the shroud of sleep as I find an all-night diner with a working payphone where I can call for a taxi home.

Home is a hot and long shower until I can no longer feel the cold and my muscles feel loose and relaxed. Home is the warmth and comfort of bed waiting for me, it's emptiness an invitation. I sleep.

I sleep through the rising sun washing the room with its light. I sleep through the morning rush of traffic and city buses and commuter trains carrying all to another workday. I sleep through children getting on school buses and old folks meeting in the park for chess. I sleep through the lengthening shadows of the sun's movement in the sky and the lunch hour rush that crowd the takeout chains.

I sleep.

***

I dream of black and white butterflies. So many of them fluttering around me with their white wings edged in black like they have been stenciled in ink. I stand still among them, watching their graceful and effortless movements. Their fragile bodies and paper-thin wings flitting with the wind.

I hold out a hand and wait with patience and stillness. In time one comes to rest delicately in my palm, wings folded. Once the creature is still, I can see up close that it is not a butterfly at all but a white piece of paper folded into an origami shape. The black on the wings is writing on the paper.

I try to grasp it in my hand, to pull apart the folds and read the writing, but once I try the paper simply turns into a burning ember in my hand and disintegrates.

I look around at the butterflies everywhere, so many of them now that the space is full of their fluttering beauty. I try to catch them in my hands; something tells me it is important that I read the messages they carry. Each time I manage to cup one between my palms they become a burning and disintegrating paper that is quickly gone.

One by one the floating origami shapes burn up slowly around me and disappear as if they never were. The messages written on the folds of their wings disintegrate with them. I am too late.

***

A darkened room. Out of the stillness and silence the sound of an African drum begins to pulse a rhythm in the dark. A dimmed light focused on a figure in the center who begins to move to the rhythm. Her head is wrapped in a black scarf and her body naked. A body moving with the beat of the drum. A body in motion, a continuous rhythmic motion. For six hours she dances and then her body tires and her movements are forced. She collapses with exhaustion on the floor.

This is what I see in my mind's eye when I think about Abramovic's 1975 performance Freeing the Body. The artist said her intention was to find that place where there is no fear of pain, no fear of death and no restrictions.

The black head scarf was meant to keep the audience from seeing the artist as a person or personality. The focus was to be on the body alone. A body free of constraint and inhibition, unbound by time. A being in connection with self and the flow of movement inspired by the drumming. A freedom to just be.

To be outside of thought. To release awareness and conscientiousness. To feel a freedom in a space and fully inhabit it with one's being. To free the body is to free the self.

***

I sit on the back deck wrapped in a knit shawl, sipping a hot mug of chamomile tea. The night is calm and has the stillness of a dream. There is only the thin sliver of a waning moon and the smog is thin enough in the sky to let the stars shine through.

I think of Marina's second performance to follow Freeing the Body; Freeing the Memory was done in 1976 in which Abramovic sat in a chair and recited every word she could remember in an effort to free herself from language. The video lasts ninety minutes until the artist can no longer remember words without repeating herself. The piece is the artist's second of the three part series by which she tries to cleanse her body and mind of consciousness. Emptying her mind of acquired words and language until the mind is a blank space encompasses the purifying process.

I name the stars by words of memory. Mother. Father. Love. The first words one acquire early in life when first learning to speak. Friend. Happiness. Comfort. Fear. Life. Death. Beauty.

The meaning of words change throughout a lifetime and become words attached to memories attached to emotions. The word 'love' can invoke warming and happy memories for one while for another memories of resentment and anger. 'Peace' may resonate with memories of comfort for one while another may struggle to remember a time when one knew what peace felt like.

I think of the word memory itself and it reminds me of the

Rorschach inkblot pictures. Look at a particular memory long enough and the shapes and colors emerge as something different from the original. A salient image remains in the mind but the details fade like a child's drawing over time.

I think about the memories that make up a life. I imagine becoming an old woman, left with only the memories created to sustain in times of loneliness. I remember reading something once about women being disproportionately affected by Alzheimer in comparison to men. I wonder what becomes of a being when the memories of a self and the life one has lived becomes a blurry and indistinct video, like a fuzzy projector of old photographs.

I look up once more to the starlight twinkling against their black canvas. I continue to name them by words of memory, wanting to store them away like a collection of loved mementos. Strength. Growth. Longing.

Night.

***

Morning brings with it the news headlines; the top story being the body of a fourteen year-old boy found hanging from a tree on the property of the middle school where he had been a student. A death by suicide. Not a statistic of the percentage of teenagers who take their own lives. Not a victim of circumstance. Not another faceless death in a city accustomed to violence. A boy who belonged to a family now grieving in the emptiness he left in his place. A child not yet old enough to have discovered all a life can hold. A young teenager overburdened with pain and not knowing how to handle it all.

I think about pain. How it's a universal feeling none can

escape on some level at some point in one's lifetime. Experienced in different ways and different depths. I think about how it can so easily be hidden by a careful mask that to all outward appearances others may never know the burden one carries within.

Pain can feel heavy as if one has been emptied out and filled with the weight of small stones. It can fill one to the point of bursting where a sharp edge cut into the flesh offers the only temporary relief. It can overwhelm the mind until the numbness of self-medicating or the use of substances is the most welcome emptiness. Pain can be a rush of adrenaline that awakens the nerves and exits the body as anger, seeking a tangible target.

Pain can wear a body and mind and spirit down. Slowly, incrementally, until one no longer feels visible to the world and the only possible escape is to look death in the face and welcome it in.

***

The cemetery is one of ancient headstones and imposing angel statues, the granite now cracked and covered in the moss and filth that claims all over the passage of time. The gate to enter is a rusted metal that creaks eerily to announce one's presence here. I have never seen anyone enter this decrepit place; the buried are too many years gone for anyone to remain who might have loved ones here.

I come to sit in the quiet of this place with a well-worn book of poetry. There is a particular old oak tree that I like to sit beneath where a small marker has been laid in the ground, separate from the rest and without the massive headstones like the others here. Out of respect for the dead with whom I share this space when I am here, I always bring fresh daisies and lay them near the marker before sitting beneath the wide expanse of the wise oak.

The trunk is sturdy and wide to lean against, like sitting back to back with an old friend who will hold one up when the tiredness of life settles deep in the bones. There is a light wind that whispers through the opening leaves and I imagine that I can understand the language of trees. The oak speaks of gentleness and serenity and I feel the solidity of its many years.

It is this feeling I imagine when I look at the pictures of Abramovic sleeping beneath the Banyan tree in Brazil. Peace and serenity captured on film for an hour of stillness in which the artist lays on the ground in a pure white robe as if asleep. She lies beneath the arching branches in the protective shade of the Banyan tree; its massive trunk standing tall and wide behind her. It is a scene of meditative serenity that emanates a soothing energy. The artist is peaceful, almost infantile, as if making herself an offering to the nature that envelopes her.

The words of Rilke are wrapped around me like a warm scarf in cold weather and I am startled when the creak of the metal gate leading into the cemetery breaks the stillness. It is my friend from Ukraine walking along the grassy footpath toward me. He is hesitant and asks if it's okay that he has come here. I don't mind and he sits in the soft grass next to me.

It is strange to hear another voice in the solitude of this place.

He gestures toward the book in my lap and recites from a passage within its pages: "I live my life in widening circles that reach out across the world. I may not ever complete the last one, but I give myself to it." He says that Rilke's earlier works were some of his best with a depth and insight that seemed lost further in his writing. He pulls a pack of smokes from his pocket and lights one, the smoke curling mystically in the air.

I take the cigarette from his hand and inhale deeply from it. We share a smoke and debate about the various poets of old, among who had the greatest impact on the world of poetry today and the depths of wisdom written so many long years before our time but that speaks of the life we live.

He passes me the smoke and I put my lips to the filter and pull. I think of life with its 'ever widening circles' and I agree with Rilke: 'I may not ever complete the last one, but I give myself to it.' Like laying myself down before the majestic Banyan tree, an offering of self in the pure white of innocence.

***

Two people sit back to back alone in a room of a gallery. A man and a woman, both with long hair that is tied together behind them. They sit like this, without an audience, without conversation, without distraction, facing opposite directions, for sixteen hours.

This man and woman are Abramovic and her partner for a piece they did in 1977 called Relation in Time. The idea behind this work was to determine what energy could be derived from an audience. The gallery opened to the public after the sixteen hours alone in silence when the two artists were exhausted and uncomfortable. They were able to continue sitting, tied together, for another hour once an audience was allowed in.

I think about the concept of energy gathered from the proximity of others and I consider the people in my life. I wonder about the energy I absorb from them and the sort they derive from me when we are each in the other's presence.

I consider my friend who has come to the cemetery and the

energy between us. I absorb from him the feeling of being protected. Of enjoyment found in the moments that make a day, unhurried and passive. Of strength. A depth of caring that emanates like the smoke unfurling from his cigarette.

I wonder what energy he feels from me. I like to think that it would be creativity, a passion for love and life and friendship. I imagine us sitting back to back without words in this stillness and I see us, one holding up the other when fatigue sets in and the idea of giving up becomes too much of a temptation.

I pick up the book in my lap and begin reading out loud the passage where I left off when he interrupted. When he reaches for my free hand I do not pull away.

***

There is a gathering of mementos and artifacts as tangible memories that one collects throughout a life. It is human nature to want to keep and even cherish possessions that have meaning in the memories they hold. Nostalgia is an innate part of humanity that is kept as photos tucked into albums and old letters stashed in boxes and items that will be kept for a lifetime.

In 2010, for the first time in the US, Abramovic's exhibition titled Private Archaeology, was displayed in New York. This intensely personal piece is of a tall wooden cabinet with a multitude of drawers. These drawers are full of photographs, handwritten letters, objects that inspired the artist's work, personal mementos and artifacts collected from around the world. One was invited to open the drawers and discover the pieces of the artist's personal life now made public.

I imagine what the drawers would hold if I were to make my own private archaeology exhibition. I think about the things that

I have kept that hold the stories of memories created. I would add the few photos I have left of my parents before the accident that took them from me. There is the book of dried and pressed flowers received from old relationships. The collages of pictures. The old birthday cards with my mother's handwriting inside that I keep in a shoebox under my bed. The scrapbook of concert tickets and gallery events and art festivals attended. Articles of Abramovic's work.

These are the things from a journey of a life created that are tangible memories I can touch and see and smell. The mementos that follow no matter how many times they are packed and moved when the nomadic restlessness in me is stirred. The things that someday will become meaningless and disposed of when I reach the end of this life.

***

The lighting is dim, the movement of water through glass reflecting patterns on the carpets which give the illusion of waves. The aquarium is mostly empty on this mid-week sunlit afternoon. Those who aren't working prefer to be enjoying outdoor activities and here is empty of the usual crowds of families with children and students on school trips.

Large sea turtles with their lazy eyes and meandering motions swim alongside brightly colored tropical fish, aimless in their artificial environment. I watch their effortless motions in the clear water as they inspect the sandy gravel on the bottom for bits of food. I remember the turtle on the riverbank and the scars carved into its shell from the blows inflicted by children. I wonder which is more unsettling, the ones encroached upon by a relentlessly growing population of humanity, or the ones held in captivity without the freedom to follow the patterns of the shifting seasons.

The manta rays float with a graceful ease, their small beady eyes watching the outside world with curiosity. They come near the glass as if seeking contact and shift away again. Their sleek black bodies and white bellies move like shadows in the water. I stand in front of the thick plate glass that separates us and the calm melancholy swimming of the rays evokes a soothing energy from within me. Like the experience of transitory objects: a physical or mental experience derived from direct interaction with a particular object.

Abramovic had constructed transitory objects based on her experience of walking the Great Wall of China. During her walk she discovered that she experienced varied energy states and realized that this variation was due to the shifting minerals in the ground. Wanting to create a similar experience for an audience, she made three objects out of copper, iron, wood and minerals. One was for sitting, one for lying, and one for standing. All three were mounted on a wall so that the one sitting, lying or standing on these transitory objects would have an interaction with the object only.

Through this exhibition the public was able to share in a physical or mental experience like Abramovic learned through the energies of the Earth's metals.

I stay with the manta rays for a long while, absorbed in their graceful energy and the peaceful calm that encompasses me in this place.

***

I kneel in the warmth of the sunlight, my hands in the rich dark soil of the garden. I like the feel of working in the dirt, the turning over of the top layer and the scooping out to make a burrow for tiny seeds that hold new growth. The grit under the fingernails connects me to the earth that sustains this life and I like the knowing that I am partaking in that sustenance. I think of the many places where the earth is barren of nutrients from the incessant over-farming and the use of artificial means to stimulate production for a demanding and ever growing population. I can almost feel the weariness and the depletion of Mother Earth as if hearing a heavy sigh in the wind.

The seeds are dry and fragile in my palm as I put them into the ground, the combination of fertile compost and soil covering them in wait for their roots to take hold. Out of the dark of the ground will come new life, reaching up through the soil toward the warmth of the light. An offering of beauty in exchange for the planting.

I think about the ugliness in the world and imagine being able to pluck out the greed and the pollution and the destruction like weeds that threaten to choke the good that has been planted. Pull them out by the twisted and tangled roots that spread like an illness and plant in their place seeds of all things beautiful and organic and life-giving.

I continue to work the ground with my hands, digging and placing and covering over until the patch of earth I have made into a garden is full of new seeds. I remove any visible sign of a weed and then I sit back to take in the work that I have done.

Now there is only the waiting. For the beautiful and the organic and the life-giving to break out of the darkness.

***

I retrieve my camera and lens ball from inside and use the setting of the backyard as a background. I set the lens ball on the ground amidst the faded leaves of last fall and lie on my stomach to capture the refracted image of sunlight on leaves and dark trees spreading their branches overhead. I capture the dark texture of the garden refracted with an open expanse of blue sky and wispy white clouds. The ivy crawling over the stonewall. I hold my fingers to the sun with the marble-size ball and capture the look of my palm holding the sun up to the sky.

The lens ball is tinted, giving the finished photos an aged look as if developed many decades ago. It is an illusion of perspective, not unlike looking at the world through a hand mirror while walking backward.

All things become the perspective from which they are seen which are as various as the ones who are perceiving. To change the way one sees the world, one image at a time, is to expand the mind beyond what is known and fosters an awakening of what has not been seen before. Old and familiar things become new and interesting again.

There is a depth to life that is barely recognized because the perspective rarely changes. So with each focus and click of my camera I create still lives of a setting that becomes changed and intricate with only a change of perspective.

***

The nights are still cool as if in remembrance of autumn but I don't mind the chill. I add layers and stay out in the gathering darkness where I can hear the tree frogs conversing and smell the faint scent of rain approaching.

There are glittering lights moving through the air, as if the glow of tiny mystical beings coming awake in the cover of night. Fireflies. It is early in the season for fireflies but I am pleasantly surprised to see their blinking glow. I think of childhood memories of running barefoot across summer grass to capture them in glass mason jars I would steal from my mother's kitchen. Once contained within the confines of the jar the lights would go out and they would remain motionless, unblinking in their captivity. It was only when they were free that they would glitter in the night like stars come down to kiss the earth.

I imagine it is the same with humanity. To be locked up in a glass jar, freedom taken away, is to snuff out the light that makes a self. To be contained for too long is to provoke madness and a slow death from the inside out. Left without the stimulation of the outside world the mind contracts and numbs. The body will atrophy and its organs will eventually give up the will to live in its failure to thrive in a natural environment.

A body needs freedom. Freedom to explore and learn and grow. A mind needs to seek knowledge and wisdom and insight. A self needs freedom to be expressive and to change and to find its place in the world it shares with other beings.

I watch the fireflies switching their lights off and on like minuscule flashlights showing them the way in the night. I know it is their freedom that makes their luminescence so beautiful.

***

The farmers' market is busy despite the mist that falls gently on the canvas awnings. Vendors crowd the park with their displays of homemade breads and pies and jam jars. The smell of fresh ground coffee beans from the organic coffee stand lingers in the air, dense and aromatic. There is the young dark skinned woman with long pulled back dreads who sells the essential oil-scented natural soap I keep on hand. I choose the jasmine and coconut today.

An older retired couple sells bouquets of flowers grown in their greenhouse and arranged in large mason jars tied with burlap bows. They are reminiscent of the sort that would live in a hippie commune with nudist meditation practices and polygamy. I buy two of their elaborate arrangements to fill my rooms with the fragrance of flowers.

An elderly woman sits alone on a hard wooden chair near the end of the park. Her tables are full of soft alpaca wool and knit woolen hats and shawls and scarves and socks. I imagine her wrinkled and bony fingers working the knitting needles to make these beautiful pieces out of the wool, massaging her stiff arthritic knuckles with a turmeric cream after hours of work.

Her posture is straight and stoic, her weathered face not unkind but not welcoming, and I think that this woman has had a hard and difficult life. She sits and watches the people moving about from table to table, her hands still and held together on her lap. She is like the portraiture of women in art in long past centuries and I long to photograph her in this place, among her alpaca wool and knitted clothing.

I think of Abramovic and the living portrait piece she did in 2009, Golden Mask. Against a black background and dressed all in black, only her head is visible. She sits still and stoic like an ancient portrait, her face covered in golden honey and gold leaf. She gazes into the camera that videos her as a living portrait for thirty minutes. The only movement is the stirring of the gold leaf mask as the air moves around her. It is hard to look away from her direct gaze which draws one closer for a better look.

I select a soft black scarf from the old woman's table and she is still silent as she reaches out for my money but her thin lips turn into a smile and she squeezes my hand a moment as if in gratitude when she takes the bills.

Although it's not cold, I wrap the scarf around me before I turn to walk home, the wool thick and warm and not unlike being wrapped in a hug.

***

Abramovic had been a performance artist for ten years in 1975. To mark the milestone she created a piece she called Role Exchange. For four hours she traded places with a prostitute who had been working for ten years as well. Abramovic spent that time in a window of the red light district in Amsterdam while the prostitute attended an exhibition opening in a gallery. The two experiences were documented by photos and film; both women took on full responsibility for what would happen in each role.

A demonstration of identity formed within the social context that women find themselves. A play on social expectations.

Not unlike my photos taken through the lens ball; a change of perspective changes ones expectations and challenges one's assumptions about social mores.

I think about the easy way by which a culture can judge and assume and pigeonhole individuals into certain roles and attach certain characteristics that identify that role. It is like an imaginative signboard worn around one's neck, as if an individual is limited to the imposed status. One's identity is formed by multiple social structures. Nature and nurture and experience and choices made and the social environment one inserts the self into. None of humanity are single-faceted.

I think about the people I pass on the busy sidewalks and I

wonder what assumptions and judgements might be made about me in passing. Is there an understanding that I am made up of many layers of a self and the face that the world sees is only the surface? Is there a realization that what is presented is not all there is, that this is only one facet of many, not unlike looking at a single side of a diamond?

***

Rain falls in steady sheets on the tin roof, its monotonous and relentless drumming invoking a lethargy that settles like a weighted blanket. With the rain comes a raw chill that climbs into the bones and we lie in my bed beneath the duvet, my Ukrainian friend and I, sharing cannoli and wine and cigarettes.

We are discussing astrology and whether the effect of the sun in its constant zodiac shifts has more effect on our energy than the moon. He is Libra, so his argument is for the sun as the planetary center and how it is known that our personalities and energies and the ways by which one expresses oneself is influenced by it. He says that is why the Greeks named their god, Apollo, for the god of light and sun because of its enormous power.

As a Gemini I argue that the moon has more pull and influence on energy. The moon is what influences our emotions and defines the subconscious part of our personality and has an effect on every one of the senses, even our memories. I emphasize that the subconscious personality is more important as that is the true underlying character of a person where one is fully and completely true to oneself. I also point out that the Greeks had a moon goddess, Selene, in their mythology; proof that the moon was viewed equally important and influential, if not more so because the moon was considered a feminine deity.

The sun and the moon. Abramovic also used these elements in her work with her partner in 1987. In a darkened room there was Abramovic to the right, wearing a plain dress, while on the left, her partner sat on a very tall chair, dressed in dark clothing. He sits motionless for the duration. A lone cello plays and with the sound of the string instrument Abramovic moves slowly, in subtle and almost imperceptible movements, from rocking forward to lifting an arm to crouching. The performance attests to traditional male and female roles and of dominance and passivity. Like the dominant light of the sun and the more passive light of the moon.

An idea comes to mind and I convince my friend to leave the warmth of my bed and come with me. We move outside, bare feet in the wet grass. We dance in the rain.

***

Scars are the remnants of a past that remind one where one has been. An attestation of a life lived. Life tells a story through the scars one bears, whether carried on the surface of the skin where they are visible to the world or held inside where old wounds are the most fragile. Scars are a testament that despite the fears, one has gone forth anyway and tasted the fruit that life bears. There is hurt found in growth, there is wounding found with love, there is pain found with entering the world. The hurt and the pain caused by the wounding eventually heal but leave a marker in its place to remind one of what has been endured.

These are the thoughts that circulate abstractedly in my mind as I watch the needle carving the soft flesh of my inner wrist. The black ink will leave a permanent marked scar, one that I have chosen to bear, the dark lettering shaping the words 'but without the dark, we'd never see the stars'.

My skin has become numb to the sting of the needle, a form of self-anesthesia that shields against the intrusion of the flesh. I feel the vibration of the needle and I wonder if it is possible to have scars without first having felt the pain of the wounding.

My body bears the visible scars of the ordinary; my right knee from a fall on gravel riding the handlebars of a friend's bike when we were children, my left wrist from a burn while working my first job at a pizza place, the thin talismans on my upper thighs from my years of cutting in high school. But there are also the invisible scars carved into my heart made by the loss of my parents at the young age of eighteen, the painful separating from my first love that was to last forever, my rejection letter to art school which I still keep after all this time hidden away in a drawer.

As one ages and matures it is the scars of life carried on the inside that bear more weight on the individual. These are the ones that bear the burden of painful memories. These are the ones that shape one's soul and form one's perspective of a life in retrospect. It is the inner wounds most often cut open again and again by the mind, forming scar tissue with each new healing.

Scars are the burden of proof that 'without the dark we'd never see the stars'.

***

It was in Scotland of 1973 where Abramovic first performed Rhythm 10. A piece that moves beyond the fear of pain and connects self to its deeper and unknown depths. A performance of art that speaks to fearlessness and recklessness and perseverance in the face of pain inflicted to the self.

The artist lays a large white roll of paper on the floor. On top of this she places ten various and very real knives. There are two tape recorders to record her movements and rhythm. She presses 'play' on the first recorder and picks up the first knife. She puts a palm to the white of the paper and with fingers spread wide she stabs between each finger as fast as she can again and again. There are sounds of pain when the knife misses the paper and knicks her skin. When a cut has been made, she sets down the knife and takes up the next one, stabbing again between her fingers. This continues until all ten knives have been used. She stops the recorder. There are bloody prints staining the paper. The artist rewinds the tape and presses play again as well as with the second recorder. She takes up the knives again, this time trying to match the cuts to the sound of the first recording.

Abramovic later told the press that during this performance she felt as if she had become a receiver and transmitter of energy; the sense of danger in the room connected her with her audience as if they had become a single organism in the here and now and nowhere else.

It is the scars of a life lived in the face of pain and despair and darkness that connect all like an invisible thread spread taut along a journey. One can follow this thread to find a way through the dark where so many have gone before.

***

The rain has stopped, the glistening wetness on new grass and the oil-slick puddles gathered on tarmac the only evidence of the days rainstorm. It is early evening and I have come to the house of my counting-the-rice-grains friend for an Ostara party. The

Spring Equinox, when there is complete balance between darkness and light, the masculine and the feminine. A time to celebrate newness and re-birth. To honor the fertility of the Earth. In the entryway of her home is a lavish altar decorated with an abundance of spring flowers, colored eggs, feathers and bowls of seeds. Symbols of new beginnings. To this altar I add the small statue of a brown hare that I have brought for this purpose, the sacred object of the lunar Goddesses. An offering of intention and respect.

The main room holds a large table with the supplies needed for all of us to weave a basket of ash wood. As the weaving begins my friend explains to us that the ash tree is seen as the link of humanity to the realms of myth and spirits. From its roots flow the sources of wisdom and fate. Ash represents the interconnectedness of all levels of existence: past, present, future, mental, physical and spiritual.

I think about the meaning of intention set forth and I wonder if this is the way to be more mindful and present in the every day. If I woke up every morning with the intention to honor what the Earth gives and to have an awareness of the way my actions effect the balance, would I do things differently? How much do I take for granted the shifting of the seasons and the knowledge that with each comes the wisdom of Mother Earth reminding us when to awaken and renew, when to harvest and gather and when to rest? An internal balance of mental, physical and spiritual that should follow the natural order of the seasons.

Once our baskets are complete and the purple fairy cocktails consumed, we move outside to the bonfire. My friend hands each of us a raw egg as we stand around the warmth of the fire. She burns a pine scented incense, its pungent sweet smell mingling with the smell of the burning wood. The egg is smooth and cool in my hand and I am aware of its fragility as I kneel with the others and bury it in the ground. The gesture is an intention for abundance and the fertility of the ground.

The ritualization is complete. All that is left now is to feast.

***

I lie in bed, full from too much food and maybe a little drunk, and I am unable to sleep. I think about rituals and why they are so important to all cultures. The elaborateness of Day of the Dead. The sacredness of the corpse washing. The sacrosanct tobacco and cleansing with sage. The dried bits of bread and tiny plastic cups of red wine. A white wedding dress. The removing of shoes outside a door. The giving of gifts to a new mother.

Ceremonies done in a particular way in a particular order. Rituals that honor, that mark milestones, that remember. A form of performance art prescribed by the custom and the occasion.

I think about rituals as a way of holding on to a history, a tangible remembering of what is important. A remembering to celebrate the momentous and joyous in life, a remembrance of those who have passed from this life, a welcoming in of new life to the world. It is important to hold on to ceremony as a remembering of what one holds as sacred and why it is so.

I think about the human tendency toward forgetting and obscuring. The meaningless motions one goes through without an understanding of why. It is not ritualism itself that is important, it is the reason for the ritual that holds the meaning. There are costumes and altars and shrines and props and prayers because humanity has become adept at forgetting. The visible and the tangible are needed reminders to reflect and remember.

I think that this is why there is the taking of the bread and the wine on Sunday. Why knees kneel before a private altar. Why a body is cleansed in preparation for burial. Why raw eggs are buried in the dirt and objects are given to honor a goddess. Because humanity needs to remember all that is sacred and important in this one life.

***

It is still early morning when I walk through the city. Businesses just beginning to open; sidewalks crowded with men and women in a hurry to get where they are headed. The streets are full of taxis and buses and cars and their exhaust and horns and music fill the air space. I walk until I reach the pier where I buy a paper cone of roasted peanuts and walk out onto the dock. I think of the wandering fisherman I met here and I wonder where he is now.

It is easier to breathe here. The water is an open horizon before me, the morning fog not completely blown out to sea yet. The lolling waves are gentle and the sound of sea birds replaces the sound of city traffic. I breathe in the smell of saltwater and imagine it cleansing the exhaust fumes and dense inner city smog from my lungs. I breathe in deeply again, I breathe out slowly. I munch on the warm peanuts and savor the salty nutty flavor on my tongue.

I sit in the quiet and watch the tide come in until the paper cone in my hand is empty. I suck the salt granules from my fingers and dispose of the trash and begin to walk away. I smell the patchouli before I see her sitting in the shade against the side of the dockhouse; an older teenager with dyed black hair and black painted fingernails. Her eyes are heavily rimmed with black liner and spread on the ground before her is an arrangement of tarot cards. She glances up and sees me watching her, asks me if I want her to do a reading for me. I tell her I'm not sure if I believe in that sort of thing and she shrugs her thin shoulders. Arranging the cards into a single pile she suggests drawing one card from the deck instead.

It is as I draw closer to her that I see the overstuffed backpack and thin blanket on the ground near her, the type that reminds me of the government-issued sort seen on prison cots. She is unkempt and unwashed. I observe all this in the time it takes her to shuffle the cards and hold them up for me to select one.

I choose the Queen of Cups. The girl remarks that this represents the nurturer; one side of the feminine spirit. The suit of the four queens are the manifestations of emotions. She points to the picture and explains that in this one the cup is closed which means that her thoughts are flowing from her subconscious mind. Looking up at me she adds that this means I must think from the depths of my soul.

I hand back the tarot, unsure of how to respond. I gesture to the collection of belongings beside her and hesitantly ask if she lives here, at the dock house. She glances down at the deck of cards and shrugs again before saying she does sometimes, when the shelters are over crowded. I ask her when she last had something to eat. There is a long silence and when I decide that she doesn't intend to answer me, I suggest that we go somewhere so I can buy her a meal.

The girl stands and fits the backpack over her shoulders, the rolled up blanket under her arm. Together, we walk toward a nearby diner.

***

Nurturer. To nurture. To care for and encourage growth. I think about the idea of nurturing as part of the feminine spirit and it reminds me of women gathered together in warm kitchens with steaming cups of coffee, sharing stories and gossip and laughter. Like the kitchen in my childhood home where my mother would leave out an after school snack and we would share milk and cookies while I told her about my day. Where my mother and father and I would have our family meals or have serious discussions.

My perception of nurturing was shaped around the heart of the home: Our kitchen. Memories were made there.

In 2009 Abramovic made a series of photos and videos titled "The Kitchen". The place was an abandoned convent in Spain and in the series Abramovic is dressed in a long black dress, her hair pulled back. She stands in the center of a run down kitchen which is barren and dirty but architecturally elaborate. Behind her is an enormous paned window which illumines the room with a pale light. In its active years this kitchen within the convent is where more than 8,000 orphans were fed. In one video, the artist stands motionless, holding a metal bowl of milk, her eyes downcast. The image is so still it appears to be a photograph until one sees the movement of the milk in the bowl from the slightest shift in her hands. Her hands tremble. The milk spills onto the black dress.

The image of the milk brings to mind a mother feeding her baby with the milk of her breasts. Giving life from her body to sustain the life she has borne into the world. I think that this must be the most basic and most instinctual form of caring for another.

Women as natural nurturers. A traditional image that links women to the history of all women. Even Eve in the garden, I think, as she was created to help take care of the earth and to raise children. To care for and encourage the growth of both.

I think again about the Queen of Cups. One side of the feminine spirit. I remember that I think from the depths of my soul and I find a strange comfort in this realization.

***

The teenage girl stands in my living room, scanning the books on my shelves. Occasionally she pulls one out, flips through its pages, and places it back. Her dark hair is wet from my shower and I think that she is a very attractive girl now that the dirt from the streets and the film in her hair has been washed away. I sense that she has a story within, a story of how she has become one of the unhoused while still such a child. But I do not ask her to tell. I do ask if she is from this area and she tells me no, that she is from a place far from where she is now. She tells me that she likes the uncertainty of each day, that she likes leaving her life up to fate and the only certainty she believes in is what she reads in the cards. She says that she is in tune with the energy of the earth and she follows this energy like a storm chaser following a tornado. Like a seeker of the elements, she says.

I have an image of this girl as a part of the repeating spiral pattern that is part of the natural world, an origin expanding outward from a single source. Not unlike a hurricane or the pattern of the galaxies. Or a snake, coiled around itself and grounded to the earth. I ask her if she knows that snakes are a symbol of primal energy in some cultures, a spiritual energy that is sourced at the base of the spine. Snakes also follow the energy patterns of the earth, no matter where they start from.

I go over to where she stands at the shelves of books and I take one with a spiral spine and black hardcover. A collection of photographs. I open it to a picture of Abramovic staring expressionless at the lens. Wrapped around her arm and neck and top of her head is a large python. Like a living crown not unlike Medusa. One of many in a series the artist did between 1990 and 1994 she titled 'Dragon Heads'. I explain that the reason the snakes never left her body or went toward the audience was because there were blocks of ice set around the artist. Snakes are cold-blooded so they would never cross the ice; instead they followed the warmth and energy of the body.

The girl studies the photo with interest and then says that maybe the snake is her spirit animal. Yes, I think, maybe so.

***

Coins clink into their slot. I press the wash button on the large industrial-size washing machine in the laundromat, watching the clothes fill with soapy water in their cyclic churning. The smell of detergents and fabric softeners linger in the nostrils like perfume. I sit with a coffee, sipping from a thick recycled paper cup.

A dark skinned woman at the machine next to mine is sorting through her pile of brightly colored clothing. She wears a red kanga and a black head scarf. Her jewelry is like a bright ocean blue; beaded and elaborate and beautiful. She separates her dark colors first and fills the machine. Her movements are quick and adept as if she has had to do this too many times.

The red of her kanga is salient against the background of white washing machines and clothes dryers and the white tile of the floor. Her movements catch my eye. Red. In her native country this symbolizes violence and sacrifice. I wonder about the wars and death and grief she lived among there. If she wears her red dress as a way of reminding herself why she has come to this foreign place where no one speaks her language and the customs are so very different from the life she knows. I wonder if she feels wrapped in memories of home; a visible reminder of a sacrifice of love for country. Blue symbolizes the importance of harmony and togetherness. Hope worn around the neck and wrists.

Red and blue. Two of the primary colors. I remember that Abramovic recognized the power in these colors, the effect they can have on the mind. She created an exercise that is not unlike the fixed meditation practices of focusing on a candle flame or the moon. In this, one sits motionless and reflectively before a square of color of one of the primary colors: red, yellow or blue. For one hour. One's psyche and physical function is influenced by color, so this meditative exercise invokes a different experience for each individual. Even Kandinsky is known to have said that 'Color is a power that directly influences the soul'.

I sip my coffee. I wait for the washing cycle to finish. I wonder to myself if color is the language of a soul.

***

Today's top news story is the overflow of displaced persons to the inner city where there is a problem of not enough housing while so many await their asylum status. A building formerly used as an assisted living facility for the elderly currently houses the asylum seekers. Homeless shelters are crowded and there is an overflow that have settled temporarily in one of the city parks. An NGO has been working diligently to hand out supplies desperately needed and to help with the application process.

I sit on the city bus looking out the grimy window, the conversations of the other passengers and the engine of the bus merging into a muted buzzing in my ears like a hovering mosquito. I step off at a stop a couple blocks from the park where some of the refugees are encamped and walk the rest of the way. It is easy to find the aid workers in their logo T shirts. I am directed to the one in charge who shows me the supplies loaded into the back of two vans that they have spent the morning unloading.

The park is full of men and women and so many children. Tents of every color dot the landscape. Clothing and blankets and trash are everywhere. The over-sized metal trash barrels are full of paper and tree limbs, makeshift fires for heat at night when the sun retracts its warmth. Many sleep, whether from boredom or lethargy or illness is not discernable. Many more sit and stare, watching the happenings around the camp.

I busy myself dispersing the cases of water, the donated blankets and sleeping bags, boxes of nonperishable food items. I am careful to not step on anything that resembles personal belongings, making my way slowly through the camp with my offerings. I want to memorize every face, the wrinkled and weathered faces of the old, the tired eyes and shoulders slumped with weariness of the younger with children they struggle to raise in this place. The ones stretched out and sleeping who are hoping to wake up to a life different from this one.

I think about the places they have left and I wonder if they will be able to stay here; to rebuild a semblance of normalcy and new beginnings where they are safe. There are many here who do not want them, who are fighting for them to be pushed out and sent away, who want to deny them the same rights by which they live because they are not of this place. I look into their faces and the kind depths of their eyes, at the children running and playing or sitting quietly with parents, at the smiles given in exchange for these simple necessities, and I admire them for what they have endured to get here. I think that their courage and inner strength and resilience is a silent message to this city. A message that says there can only be renewal with the choice to rise from the ashes.

***

I am up late into the night, my mind swirling with the remnants of stories told by the displaced ones I talked to today. Their voices and fragments of their journeys weave together like a multi-fabric tapestry in my memory.

I sit outside, surrounded by the night. I smoke and drink wine from the bottle. I think about roots and rituals and customs attached to a place that are imprinted upon a being as one comes into the world. A part of one's identity is formed by heritage and history and ancestry. Knowing where one's roots originated and where one is from is food for the spirit.

I think about the ones forced to sever those roots that connect one to a place; the ones who forfeit their customary lifestyle to ensure survival by coming to a country that is unknown and unwelcoming. The ones homesick for the land they love who have sacrificed all for a chance to be free and safe. I wonder if anything would change if the media coverage brought awareness to the genocide and the beatings and the rapes and the corruptness of the governments that the displaced have escaped from. I wonder if anything would change if there was knowledge of the ones left behind, wounded and sick and the knowing that resources for medical attention are scarce or unsanitary.

Safety. Doctors. Jobs. Stability. Things that are taken for granted in this place. There is a crying out against asylum seekers, a resentment that seeks to deport all back to the suffering and violence as if the displaced are non-human and vetoed of civil rights.

I think about the casual way it is said that there is no price that can measure a human being's worth, yet I realize in a starkly clear way that the worth of another is determined by the roots of one's origin.

***

In a milky colored sky there are black wings soaring on the current of air beneath them; I can hear the loud cries of so many crows. I can hear the weight of their wings when they flutter. They are in a strange formation, hovering and circling and calling above. I am drawn to their movements. I stand with my camera poised and capture their flight. I have never seen so many together. They seem to be like black stars in a white sky.

I hear a soft thud on the ground behind me. I turn to look and a crow has fallen in the grass, dead. I can see up close the glossy shine of its feathers, the sky reflected in its lifeless black eye. I crouch and photograph the body.

As I stand, I hear another fall twenty feet away. It too is lifeless. I look up to the sky and see the black wings falling one by one. Their bodies hit the ground like large hail stones, feathers covering the grass in my yard. I am stunned, the sensation of a bad omen moving toward me.

I give up trying to photograph the birds and move into the safety of the house. I watch through the window until they start flying into the glass. I can hear them bouncing off every window of every room. I move through the rooms, pulling the curtains closed. I sit on the floor, hands over my ears to block out their screams.

So many wings. So much screaming. I want it to stop but I don't know how to do so. I scream, trying to make my voice louder than their sounds.

I wake myself screaming in the darkness.

***

It is afternoon. I am leaving the inner city park after volunteering again; sorting through clothing donations and passing out sweatshirts and pants and sandals. Instead of catching the bus toward home I walk around for a while. I follow a tarmac jogging path that stops at the end of an avenue. A small rundown white church sits on the corner, clearly shut down and abandoned for some time. Its quaint architecture doesn't fit in with the city buildings that crowd it but there is still something about it that draws me.

I dig my camera from my bag and photograph the church. It's crumbling stone steps and weathered steeple. The faded and peeling white paint and the trim that hangs loose above the foundation. I move closer, capturing the emptiness of the windows. I can't photograph the sense of sadness I feel here.

Maybe this is what moves me to the double front doors, the latch opening reluctantly to a dark and cold interior.

Layers of thick dust coat the wooden floor that creaks under my weight as I move around the space. The pews or chairs that once were here to seat the faithful have been removed, there is only a large empty room and the altar. There is still a life size wooden cross hung high on the wall behind the pulpit and a statue of the crucified Christ upon it.

An abandoned religion I think as I approach the cross to study the statue closer. The crown of thorns set into the scalp, blood trickling down the sides of the painted face. Eyes closed in death. The nails in the hands. The wound in the side. The nails in the feet. I photograph the statue with its chipping enamel and coating of dust.

I can almost hear the echoes of the hymns that were sung here. The prayers recited. Religion as a hope to cling to.

My shoes leave prints in the dust and I crouch near the floor, using my finger to draw my name in the filmy grit like a prayer.

I walk out into the light of the afternoon and turn in the direction of the bus stop.

***

In 1984 a photograph was made. The object is a large and steep craggy rock. Abramovic climbs up the left side in a long black dress and sneakers, her face looking up to the top as she holds her body to the rock. Her partner is on the right side, wearing light colored clothing and also looking up toward the peak. The rock stands solid between them. The only way to reach each other is to keep climbing. The photograph has been printed in a way that Abramovic's partner is upside down as if climbing down instead of up. They called this work Tra tan Tra. Translated this means 'Between tan Between Between.'

There is always difficulty, always an obstacle to be maneuvered. Life is messy and hard and sometimes feels like a steep climb to nowhere. I think that sometimes the only thing that can be done is to hold on to a crevice and keep the feet firm on the solidity of the rock. To have one alongside to join in the climb and meet at the top is what keeps one moving upward, one handhold, one step up, at a time. The difficulty becomes worthwhile when standing on the peak and taking in the view together.

We sit on my living room floor, eating Chinese takeout picnic-style. My Ukrainian friend has brought over some of my favorites: moo goo gai pan, eggrolls, sake. We eat with the wooden chopsticks, clumsily, laughing at each other's attempts. It is nice to hear the sound of his laughter; his mother has been sick and with the air spaces shut down near Poland and Ukraine he is not able to fly to be with her.

Spread around us are the final edited prints of my photographs. The photos taken in my yard with the lens ball. The photos of the abandoned church. He tells me that I have a gift, a way of seeing the world in a way that most people don't. He holds the photo of the dust covered crucifix and the Christ. He asks me if I was ever religious.

I concentrate on twirling the noodles around the chopsticks while I consider the question. I tell him I have never believed in the idea of religion itself. I believe in kindness and love and putting good into the universe, I believe there is life after death for those who make the most of this life. I don't believe in labeling beliefs with religious titles. I also understand the human need to have hope in something greater, something that gives the ordinary life meaning and purpose.

He sets the photo down again, considering my response. I think of the childhood he has shared with me, the stories of going weekly to the mosque and the daily prayers recited, and I see us as two on opposite sides of the steep rock face. I am the dark and he is the light and although our starting points were continents apart, we are now making the climb together for a better view.

I feel his fingers, gentle and warm, on my face. He moves aside the hair that has fallen over my cheek, brushing it behind my ear. His hand lingers.

***

I sit on the subway, the plastic molded seat hard and uncomfortable. A small cloth doll with yarn hair and bead eyes that fits in the palm of my hand. A gift from one of the children at the inner city park. I run my finger over the cloth face and the burlap dress, thinking of the innocence of children. The trusting nature and unblemished perception of the world one inhabits.

In 1977 Abramovic and her partner performed 'Balance Proof' in Switzerland. The artists stood nude facing each other with a double-sided mirror between them. The mirror was taller than both of them, their bodies on either side keeping the mirror in perfect balance. For thirty minutes they stand, surrounded by an audience and uncertain through the duration that the other is still on the other side. If one steps away the mirror will fall. It is Abramovic who steps back first at the half hour mark. Without her weight to balance the glass the mirror crashes to the floor and breaks.

The trust of a child is not unlike this. They will stand firm on one side of the mirror with complete trust that another is on the other side to keep balance. At the same time they are as fragile as the mirror itself; once the trust is broken they are shattered.

Children are thrust into the cold world cocooned in trust and innocence. I think to myself as I look at the small gift I hold, that it is the adults that take away their innocence. They are born into a world that is in a hurry for them to grow up. They are born to a world that steps away from the mirror before they have learned to be balance proof.

***

I walk the rest of the way to the farmhouse that has an old barn converted to a honey store. Wooden shelves and tables with jars of dark honey and beeswax candles and lip balms and lotions. It is this place where I come for fresh honey and lotion. Although now that I am here I see the barn doors are locked and the handwritten 'Closed' sign is perched in a front window.

I walk around the side of the barn to the open field where the hives are. I can see the bees hovering in the light and there is the beekeeper, carefully removing the combs with slow efficient movements before putting the lid of the hive back in place. She sees me standing to the side and waves with recognition.

She carries the large jar of fresh honeycombs and walks over to meet me. She is veiled with her protective netted hat, quick to apologize for the closed sign but explains that she has been behind in production of the honey and has had difficulty meeting the demand. She is willing to let me in for my usual purchases.

She leaves the sticky jar and her hat in a storage shed and walks around to let me in the store. I pick out my honey and lotion and balms, setting them on the wooden counter to retrieve the money from my bag. I am surprised that the bees are able to survive the cold winters. The beekeeper smiles knowingly and tells me their secrets. She says that when winter approaches and food becomes scarce the worker bees will force out the drones, the male bees, and prevent them from returning which means they will eventually starve. During the cold months of winter the remaining bees will form a tight cluster ball, the worker bees vibrating their flight muscles to generate heat. The beekeeper says that it is all a delicate balance of ensuring the survival of the queen bee and her brood.

Yes, I agree, a delicate balance to ensure the survival and

growth of the youngest within the hive. The thought crosses my mind as I say goodbye and walk back toward the subway station, if only humans would learn to do the same.

***

I pour the dark rich and sweet honey into the ingredients that will make bread. I catch some on the tip of my finger and lick its sweetness while I proof the yeast. I think about the honey bees travelling far to find their nectar and pollen to bring back to the hive. The efficiency by which they work, transferring the nectar mouth to mouth within the hive to reduce the moisture content which turns the nectar into honey. The honey is placed in storage cells and capped with beeswax. Before the worker bee leaves the hive for more nectar, she cleans and combs herself so her work will be more efficient.

I add the flour little by little, working it into the dough until the consistency is just right and ready for the kneading. I think about the danger to honeybees' existence as more and more of the wild flowers and plants they search for to find nectar and pollen are removed as the human population expands. There is the problem of pesticide use that is toxic when ingested by the worker bees. The change in climate as well is disruptive as this effects the timing of the seasonal flowers blooming and the honeybees' nesting behavior.

My hands sink into the elastic sticky dough, kneading and turning and kneading its soft flesh. I think about the loss of the honeybee, what a world without their existence would be. A collapse in the ecosystems. A lack of pollination of the fruits, nuts, grains and vegetables that support the lives of the human population. I think about the interconnectedness of life, the delicate cycle that exists despite the ignorance of it. The small honeybees have a life-size impact on the life of humanity and the actions of humanity are impacting the lives of the bees.

    I set the bread dough in a large bowl and cover it with a dishtowel for the first rise. Bread that feeds the body. The sweetness of the honey given forth as an offering from the bees. A delicate partnership of life supporting life.

***

The sun sets, a soft glow settling over newly green grass and lengthening shadows created by the tall maples and black birch. Pink and orange shade the horizon like a child's water colors.

    A plate of sliced bread drizzled with honey sits between us, my counting-the-rice-grains friend and I, as we sit on the steps of the deck soaking up the last warmth of daylight. I eat of the moist bread, dabbing pieces into the honey that has pooled on the plate.

    My friend is newly pregnant. She is afraid and unhappy, this woman nearing forty, who has lived her life defining freedom as being childless. Once, in her last year of graduate school, she tells me that she had an abortion then. The pain and sickness endured as her body expelled the fetus, is not something she has easily lived with since. This time she will submit to the inevitability. She lets herself be vulnerable, her tears clogging her throat.

    The air has grown cold as night approaches. We go inside. I go into the bathroom and draw a hot bath, a drop or two of lavender oil added for comfort. I take off her sweater and unclip her bra, letting it slip off to the floor. I push her jeans and underwear down over her hips and thighs. I strip myself naked as well and we sit together in the bath, my legs wrapped around her waist and my arms cradling her to my chest. This delicate yet strong body that is carefully knitting together a new human being within the unseen womb. Her breasts are already swollen and tender, her body just beginning to learn the changes necessary to support a new life.

We sit. She cries.

***

In 1976, 'Talking About Similarity' took place in Amsterdam. The performance begins with Abramovic's partner in the center while the audience looks on. He sits with his mouth open, the only sound the sucking of saliva. This goes on for the first half of the performance. Then he closes his mouth and takes up a needle and white thread. With lips pressed together he pierces his bottom lip with the needle until it breaks through the skin inside his lip. He then pierces his top lip through with the needle, pulling through the white thread until he has literally sewn his lips together. He ties two knots in the thread. He sits for a time like this and then disappears from the stage. Abramovic moves to the center, taking her partners place. She answers the questions from the audience, speaking as if she is him and they are one. Her partner's silence is the basis of the performance. With his mouth closed by force he can no longer decide himself when to speak. He has, in effect, taken away the choice and she begins where he left off, giving him a voice. Their roles are interchangeable.

He is the performance, she is his voice and his thoughts. They are two parts of one whole.

***

I have come back to the old cemetery with the creaky metal gate.

The sun is warm on the body, an invitation to be outdoors. I set the daisies on the grave marker near my usual spot under the large oak. This time I have brought my camera so I can photograph some of the oldest and crumbling tombstones. I meander around the stones, barefoot in sun-warmed grass. Occasionally I kneel near a grave stone that I find intriguing: black mold climbing over the face, the statue of a cherub with half its face broken away and the other half cracked as if it had been broken and carefully glued back together. Another grave is dated with a birth: 1881, but the date of death is left unmarked. An angel statue with wings spread wide and eyes downcast toward the grave stands on the tombstone as its guardian. I photograph the stone with the angel poised above. Then I photograph half the face of the statue, one wing and one half the body.

I take my time, looking at dates and inscriptions that are so aged it is hard to make out the words. Something moves in the grass as I near a grave at the edge of the cemetery. A garter snake, its coloring blending almost imperceptibly with its surroundings, moves silently away from me. Its body is beautiful and graceful in the low grass. I think that the vibrations of my body moving toward the warm stone where it laid coiled in the sun must have scared it away.

I set down the camera in the grass and gently pick up the snake, wrapping its smooth body around my arm. Its small head in my hand reaches away from me, tongue flickering the air. Its small beady black eyes are disinterested. I take in the coloring of the brown skin, edged in yellow with a lighter belly. This harmless creature that invokes fear in so many. I wonder if humanity's ophidiophobia started in the Garden of Good and Evil when the snake was first viewed as a being to be feared of. Or is this common fear something that has been passed down like an old wife's tale? I remember the unhoused teenager with the tarot cards. How she thought maybe the snake was her spirit animal. I think too of Abramovic and her performances with snakes, her desire to eradicate a negative mindset toward these necessary animals and reorient a people to a way of thinking reminiscent of cultures which saw snakes as healers. A people who would perform snake dances while handling these creatures as a celebration of fertility before releasing them into the fields to ensure good crops for the season. Some viewed snakes as a symbol of an umbilical cord, one that binds humanity to the earth.

Abramovic and her partner did a performance in Germany in 1978 called Three, in reference to the third 'performer', a snake which lay on the floor between them. The artists directed vibrations at the snake by blowing over the top of a bottle or plucking a taut wire. They laid flat on the floor on their bellies in similar fashion to the animal, using the vibrations to stimulate the snake to respond to one or the other. In the video the snake is drawn to Abramovic as she plucks the wire, moving toward her in a slow rhythmic motion, head raised and tongue flickering. The artist tries to communicate with the snake by mimicking its movements.

The garter snake in my hands reaches down toward the safety of the ground, and I lean down to release it gently into the grass. A prayer of renewal for the humans bound to this place by the symbolic umbilical cord that slithers away.

***

With photo prints and supplies scattered around me on the floor I attempt to put together a photo collage from pictures taken at the old church and the cemetery. The television is playing a documentary about ancient ruins and temples in faraway countries; a story I am not really following as I work until there is discussion about the vandalism of sacred ruins sites.

A temple more than three thousand years old that once stood as a temple for the god of the moon. Researchers had found more than three hundred slabs at this site with inscriptions of an ancient language no longer spoken today. Now, walking around the site where this temple once stood in honor of a god worshipped and considered sacrosanct, these three thousand year-old slabs lay on the ground among discarded plastic bottles and other pieces of trash. The slabs have been smeared over with ink.

I think about the devastation of this site, the degradation enacted upon a history. A smearing over of a civilization that hold the origins of all that have existed in that place since. A way of life, ritual, custom, and religion desiccated by a population uncaring and without respect for one's own history of a people and place. It is important, I think, to know the significance of the place one occupies, to understand what has come before in order to keep the history relevant to life in the present.

Thailand, 1983. Abramovic and her partner combine performance art and photos into a video, representative of a people and a culture. A panoramic video image moves slowly over a shirtless teenage boy lying on the grass, hands resting behind his head, asleep. Near the boy's head lies an older man dressed in a traditional orange robe, on his stomach in the grass, asleep. A woman on her side, sleeping in a pink garment. A young boy, lying still and quiet, seemingly asleep until his eyes open to gaze direct at the camera watching him. The video becomes a series of still images, illustrating a culture and custom of Thai people. The images linger for half the twenty minute span of the video, imprinting on the mind a memory of a people removed from the modernity of the world. The video ends with an aerial panoramic view of men and women again spread out on the ground as if to signify the end of a culture. The end of a way of life.

This collective was called City of Angels. An embodiment of tradition and the spirit of a known history. Abramovic's partner wrote, in regards to this work, "To have the most original moment of a culture represented as a living being."

I study the video on my screen of the temple site littered with trash. A site that holds the most original moment of a culture.

***

We sit outside the clinic in the back of a taxi, the brick building tall and imposing and formidable next to us. My friend sits next to me, her calmness and energy I try to absorb as I wait for her to be ready in the face of her first ultrasound. She takes a deep breath and meets my eyes, saying that this will make it all real, seeing this developing fetus with its beating heart protected within her womb. She glances at the multi-floored building with its suite number clearly stenciled on the front door. She tells me that she has been trying to choose a gender neutral name so she can more easily associate this pregnancy with a tiny living human once it has a name. Because a name is important.

A name has meaning. A name gives one identity. I think about my own name, a name of Gaelic origin that means "wise". A name sets one apart as an individual. Time and intention are given to the choice of a name, the permanence of it a solemn responsibility. I wonder too if a personality grows to become the meaning of a name or is it a subconscious doing when one embodies the spirit of it? I think of the ones who go through the arduous process of changing a name to one that identifies more with who one feels the self to be as an individual and I know what my friend says is true: A name is important. Maybe the most important thing a person identifies with throughout a lifetime.

    She opens the door of the taxi, stepping out onto the curb. I lean forward to pay the driver before climbing out behind her. Behind us, we hear the taxi pull away and merge again into the flow of traffic. I take her hand, small and soft and cool, in my own. We walk inside.

***

I sit on the wooden footbridge overlooking the river. I slip off my sandals and dangle bare legs over the water. I photograph the way water parts around rock in the current. The gnats that hover near the surface like a moving iridescent cloud in the glow of the sun. I can see the shine of light refracting off a discarded beer bottle on the river bottom. Other pieces of indiscernible trash that have sunk below the moving water and in my mind I imagine the ones that come here in the late hours to smoke and drink, leaving evidence of their presence here like a footprint in cement.

    A ladybug on the sun warmed wood, blood red body with telltale black polka dots and tiny thin black legs. Her shell opens to reveal translucent minuscule wings as if ready to fly away, then closes. I set my finger on the wood, letting her climb onto the tip where I can lift her up for a closer look. She marches purposefully across my palm, her movements hardly a tickle on my skin, so light and so fragile. Her wings expand once more and she is gone, following an unknown scent. Another ladybug, this one still and lifeless, lies on its back near a pylon. The sight of it reminds me of something I once read although I can't remember where I came upon the information. I remember that if one were to find a dead ladybug, insect or animal, that one should honor the death respectfully with a prayer or a burial. It is believed that once something has passed it takes on an interest in what happens to the body it has left behind. This belief is the foundation of spiritual traditions across cultures and countries that honor the vacated bodies.

I scoop the ladybug into my palm and carry it away from the bridge. There is a nearby patch of spring violets where I create a small indentation in the dirt and place the bug in its mini grave. A way to honor the death respectfully.

***

A video pans the room of a Sicilian living area where four or five women dressed in black with black veils over their hair sit in solemn silence. Women in mourning. Hands folded together in laps, ankles crossed. All as still and silent as if looking at a photograph. Sicilian men are outdoors, stoically composed.

The video is a collaborative work made by Abramovic and her partner in 1984 titled 'Terra degli dea madre'. The focus of this piece was a look at role patterns during a period of mourning, part of the artists' focus at that time exploring the relation between men and women.

I consider the ways a culture grieves and despite closing the gap between gender differences there still remains imposed expectations. I see a society that expects its boys and men to be strong and stoic in the face of death. Emotion and grieving openly shows weakness and vulnerability. A culture that has taught this gender to internalize feelings, to swallow down the pain and not allow the self to show that its hurting. While the men and boys learn to grieve in private, the women and girls are expected to grieve openly. Weeping and wailing and visible distress are the acceptable signs of appropriate mourning. Too little emotion for too short a time evokes a sense of not being upset enough and can seem cold and uncaring.

In Sicily it was not uncommon at one time for a grieving family to 'hire' wailers in order to show the socially appropriate amount of mourning.

I remember the period of grief and mourning in the wake of my parents' deaths. A time when I became so empty of emotion that I was unable to cry for them. Days that passed in a blur, the world moving forward while I felt as if time had frozen. Sleep was my only comfort then.

Mourning is personal. Mourning is felt in the fabric of a soul. Grief can be messy and it can be stoic. It is gender blind. It can be passive or it can be stormy or somewhere in between at different times and on different days. But it cannot be prescribed.

***

I sit at the edge of the park smoking a cigarette. Nearby is the remains of an old tree the city officials had taken down because it had become so rotted it was weak. Heartrot. Damage to the protective bark had left open wounds for fungi to enter and decay the wood. Like the carving of names and initials into the bark that can damage the tree cells and cause it to starve to death. An invisible dying that starts at the heart center and spreads like illness.

I stub out the smoke in the dirt and take a closer look at the stump that testifies to the life that once was here. My fingers touch the rings of the wood, markers of growth and age. In places where the rot has not spread I try to figure the age of this tree, roughly one hundred, a few years more.

The Prometheus tree was thought to be the oldest living tree until it was accidentally cut down in 1964 by a man who had gotten his tree corer stuck in it. A park ranger helped him cut the tree down to remove the tool. It was only then, when they began counting the rings of the tree, that it was discovered to be the oldest living bristlecone pine at more than five thousand years old.

I think about the endurance of this tree, the ability to continue to grow and thrive despite harsh winter storms and fire. The ability to seal off a wound to prevent further damage and grow around it. The decades of changes and technology and population witnessed in its lifetime. The stories contained within its deadened cells.

I feel the heartrot at its center, its wounds brought upon by human hands. I think about humanity's ability for destruction and wonder if it knows any limit.

***

A photograph taken in 1984. An aerial view above the wide blue expanse of the sea, a dark and deep royal blue of endless depth. At the center the two artists float on the surface, nude, head to feet, the water rippling out in widening circles as if it is from these two that everything radiates from. A picture of freedom. As if nothing else exists except each other. Nothing else matters, nothing else can touch this moment of pure existence.

In this room there is silence that surrounds. I lie in his bed, our clothes discarded on the floor near us. We face one another, he sleeps and I watch him sleeping. I am wrapped in the warmth and the scent of him, like evergreen and Downy and cigarettes. He is still in his sleep, his body hardly moving with each breath. His eyes closed, his mind in a dream world where I cannot follow. I trace a finger lightly through his hair, the curve of his cheek and chin, the outline of his lips, his chest.

Earlier we had lain here with our voices filling the quiet. We talked about the progression of the war in Ukraine, his mother's perseverance in the face of illness, his hope that one day his parents will be able to come here. I think of a hard cover book, its pages stained red with blood. Abramovic demonstrated the imprint of war upon a people when she placed a plastic bag containing two compartments on a flat white surface. In one part was red liquid like blood and the other had a white hard cover book of family photos. The artist slit open the parts of the plastic together so that the red blood seeped out onto the book and Abramovic's hands. As she picks up the book and flips through its pages the pictures become smeared and stained with the blood. It cannot be washed away. In the same way, there is no way to undo the damage that this war has already inflicted.

With eyes still closed he reaches for me, entwining my hair in his fingers. Nothing exists in this moment aside from the two of us. Nothing else can touch this moment of pure existence.

***

A moonless night. I take the subway home, having left his bed and tiptoeing out while he slept. A note on the pillow for morning. The subway is nearly empty, the harsh lighting casting a sickly pall on the faces of those who sit quietly heading into the night. I try to imagine the places they might be going to and the places where they were before. Now, here, riding this subway in the middle of the night, this is a fleeting moment of paths intersecting at the same time in the same place that will never happen again.

I fall asleep, lulled by the movement and the tiredness that has settled in. I dream of an empty beach at the ocean's edge. It is windy and it is cold. Waves rush to the shoreline; whitecaps roll farther out where the water is deep. I am walking although I don't know where I am headed. There is nothing and no one in sight. I do not recognize this place. But I am certain that I am walking in the right direction. I see something ahead of me on the beach, lying so near the water that the waves touch it. A seal, I think. Until I draw near enough to see that it is a person, stretched out on her back in the sand. This woman is Abramovic, dressed in black, her hair wet from the water that caresses her. Her eyes are closed, face upturned to the sky as if it is a hot summer day. Her head follows the movement of the water, her muscles and limbs so relaxed in her meditative state that the elements move her.

I wake when the subway comes to a stop, the brakes loudly announcing its presence at the station. I begin the short walk home, thinking of Stromboli, the video performance of Abramovic on the beach that I dreamt of. The work is representative of the artist giving her body to the influence of external forces. A state of complete mental abandon. The beach was in Sicily, the work filmed in 2002.

I arrive home and go to the bedroom without turning on a light. I strip my clothes off once more and climb beneath the covers, quickly and effortlessly giving my body over to the influence of sleep. A state of complete mental abandon.

***

The park has been transformed into a collection of tents and booths and displays. Art in its various forms fills the expanse for the annual 'Art in the Park' weekend. Photography. Abstract paintings. Landscapes. Jewelry. Contemporary paintings. Expressionist paintings. Vendors selling bottles of water or hot coffee.

I work my way through each booth browsing, looking, admiring, making conversation with some of the artists. I like to know what inspires one to create certain images with certain colors and the meaning within the frames. A life size painting captivates me and I linger, contemplating. A silhouette of a woman, long hair caught on an imaginary wind, large wings like those of an angel unfolded and expanded. A work so simple yet so visually compelling.

The last table is where a gentleman sits, supplies and blank canvases at the ready. A cheap price for a self-portrait if I have time to sit. I sit across from him while he sets up a canvas on an easel and selects his tools. He is a retired art professor. He spends most of his time in his studio now, painting landscapes. He loves creating portraits, the work of capturing the essence of an individual. He tells me all this while his eyes study my face, his hand working quickly and broadly over the canvas.

He takes the canvas from the easel and turns it for me to see. A pencil and charcoal drawing startling in its likeness. A whimsical expression captured in my eyes, full lips with a hint of a smile as if holding a secret. It is the butterfly that holds my attention, a black and white butterfly that hovers over my shoulder. I remember my dream. The origami butterflies with the black ink messages.

The artist wraps the portrait in delicate tissue paper wrapping before I leave. I hesitate, holding the package against my chest. I ask him what inspired him to add the butterfly in my drawing. He says that butterflies represent transformation, from something small and grounded to the earth into something beautiful and free, that he sensed instinctually a similar metamorphosis within me.

Metamorphosis. The change of one form into another. From grounded to free.

***

An empty room in a gallery. A steel stage in the center. Lined up around the perimeter of the staging are ten pairs of shoes. Empty. Waiting. Projected on the wall behind the stage a video plays. A woman, alone, dancing the mambo on the same steel stage as the one in the gallery. She dances in red high heels, her energy reaching through the video, an invitation to slip on the magnetized shoes and dance alongside her.

Mambo was done in 2003, in Italy. Abramovic danced in an empty mental hospital wearing magnetized heels on steel staging, the movements requiring more effort and energy as she worked against the pull of the magnetic force beneath her feet. The artist believed that she and her audience could reciprocate energy by inviting the audience, through the use of video and objects, to dance with a projected image of herself.

I sit among friends at a corner table in a coffee lounge. The lighting is dim, creating a hushed and amicable atmosphere as I sip a hot macchiato. It is Poetry Night here, the lounge is crowded with writers waiting their turn to share, sipping glass drinks of liquid courage. Poetry fans and friends of the writers fill the tables and couches around the room. Voices hush as the readings begin, the artists voices and the clink of ice against glass and the scraping of a chair against the wooden floor become the only sounds.

There is a reciprocation of energy that takes place here. The language and emotion of the writings filling the space, the audience's expectation and reaction in response. I realize that this is not so different from performance art, there is interpretation and acting and a give and take interaction with the listeners that in effect transforms the audience into participants through emotional engagement.

I sit and sip and listen. I let myself become energy, a willing participant in the performance. Like slipping on the magnetized shoes and dancing on the stage.

***

A wine glass half full with water set on an unfolded white linen napkin. A blank white wall space provides the backdrop for the photograph. A medicine dropper of vibrant blue ink. I squeeze a drop of ink into the water. Photograph the way the ink swirls and spreads, tendrils of blue bleeding through the clear. Another drop of ink into water. I photograph the way the ink looks like blue veins, spreading and reaching and branching. Like a cancer that spreads through the body. Like the pollution that seeps into the oceans.

Like an infection that eats away at the soul.

I add droplets of ink, photographing each stage as the water becomes translucent blue. I think about a soul, the core of an individual where one derives the truest self. I think about an infected soul, infected by biases of a culture. An infection of immorality. Of materialism. Of false media. An infection that leads one to believe happiness is found in the external. A slow, insidious disease that resides unfelt and unseen but spreads like ink in water, staining and turning what is clear and what is pure into something dark. Something that cannot be undone. An inkblot that stains the fabric of humanity.

***

Touch is the most intimate of the senses. A sense of engaging with another, a form of sensory memory that lingers in the skin. Like a photograph taken with fingers and lips as the lens. I feel his hand, warm and calloused and soft all at once, as he traces the outline of my body from the roundness of my breast to the hollow of my stomach to the curve of my hip. Like drawing a map of a place to be remembered and revisited. His lips follow the lines traced by his fingers and I wonder if I have ever felt this sensuousness of my femininity like I do in this moment. Not unlike the feeling one experiences during the golden hour of the day, when the sun is setting and bathes everything in its ethereal golden light. Or seeing the moon eclipse the sun, a brilliant play of shadow and light.

Later, I will wonder about what it means to be feminine beyond just the characteristics associated with being a woman. Is one's femininity conscribed by the curves of a body, an embodiment of sensuality, a certain way one clothes the body? I will ponder the way a culture has marketed femininity, misleading the female sex to believe that it is a certain body image, a certain level of provocative, a certain way of using one's body that defines being feminine.

Later, I will remember Abramovic's 1998 video, Red Period, a performance of the facets of being feminine. The video is made with red tones, the color associated with love and passion and the prostitutes of the Red Light District who would use the red light to conceal identity and, at the same time, to look more appealing. In the video the artist is seen close up, her face the focus as she gazes longingly at the camera. Her painted lips are a seductive and inviting half-smile. She raises one hand, her index finger beckoning the viewer in a playful manner. She stops luring and moves her finger back and forth in front of her face as if to say 'off limit'. The video fades to black, comes back into view showing the artist's eyes at the bottom of the screen. She looks up, running her hands over her face and pulling at her hair in a girly fashion. Then she looks at the camera again, her eyes and lips once more seductive and playful. The video fades to black.

 I will think of all this much later. For now, there is only him and me and this moment, a brilliant play of shadow and light.

***

We go out once darkness has enclosed all in its sleepy embrace. A crowded and noisy pub with sticky tabletops and cold beer poured into chilled glasses. Someone puts a bowl of free peanuts on our table and we busy our hands with the shelling, popping the nuts into our mouths and piling the brittle and dry shells in the center. He says that it reminds him of a childhood game he used to play with friends back home, Edible/Inedible. One would hold a ball, one of those shiny and colorful bouncy ones that used to be sold in Walmart, and call out the name of an object as the ball is tossed randomly to another player. If the object is edible then the player catches the ball. If it is inedible then the player lets the ball drop. The faster it is played the more challenging it becomes.

I drink the dark beer, feeling the foam on my upper lip. I wipe my mouth with my hand and I remember out loud games played with neighborhood children. Simple games like tag and hopscotch and dodgeball. I remark that now it is rare for children to play outside. Instead of the innocence of imaginative play there is now electronic entertainment that leaves no room for creative play and dulls the imagination instead of fostering it.

I reach for a handful of peanuts to be shelled, my nail piercing into the outer layer and breaking it away to reveal the small nut enclosed within. I tell him about the work Abramovic did in 1986 where a handful of children were filmed at MIT using computer graphic equipment. The video was like a social experiment to encourage thinking whether technology is manipulative or benign. The idea seems more relevant in current culture than it did in 1986 but seems widely disregarded now.

He says that society has lost its children. They have become absorbed into a culture that we no longer recognize. I drain my glass, playing the words over in my mind. The lost children. Like an unreachable Neverland adults can never enter. A place of innocence lost instead of innocence everlasting.

***

The morning is clear and warm, the sun bathing all it touches as if beckoning one to come outside. The sky is washed in a baby blue watercolor. The sort of morning one would see illustrated in a children's book. I walk the sidewalk barefoot, rubber sandals in hand, so I can feel the warmth of the bricks on my skin. It is the same warm comfort as standing near a bonfire on a cold autumn night.

I meet her at the playground that was once defaced with

graffiti on its cement walls. Children are in school so there are only a handful of parents with toddlers in the sandboxes and on the slides. She sits on a swing, idly rocking back and forth as she watches the babies with their sippy cups and fistfuls of goldfish crackers. I understand, without her saying it, why she wanted to come here. I can see it in her eyes, the glimmer of a future she is reluctant to embrace.

I sit on the empty swing next to her, my toes in the hollowed out dirt where so many little feet have dug in and scuffed the earth. The chain link metal is cold as I wrap my hands around them and I swing lightly, remembering the dizzying heights I would jump from as a child at recess.

She tells me the name of the baby. A name that means distinguished; revered. I try to imagine what she will look like when her body is swollen and weary with pregnancy, the intimate moments spent with babe to breast and the nights spent pacing in an effort to soothe a little one to sleep. The pieces do not fit in my mind, like trying to fit together a puzzle with mismatched pieces.

I think about motherhood and an image of roots growing, spreading and branching fills my mind. A symbol of permanency. Of being grounded. Stagnant. I think about creative energy becoming staunched, transformed into energy required to nourish the roots. The feeling is not unlike the soul being torn away from the body it inhabits. I instinctively want to dig up the roots, to burn away any possibility of permanency.

I want to remain rootless.

***

Abramovic kneels on the ground, knees in the dirt, sitting on her heels. Her long black hair is pulled back into a low ponytail. She wears a full sleeve black shirt and black pants. Feet bare. She kneels before a sad-eyed donkey, still and poised as it faces her. The artist holds the gaze of the animal as if sharing an intimate moment with an old friend. There is a sense of something being exchanged from one to the other, something spiritual and calming. In the video, which Abramovic titled 'Confession', a text appears like a subtitle sharing pieces of the artist's childhood memories and anecdotes although she is not physically speaking throughout the piece.

I think about the meaning of confession. To admit or acknowledge. I think about wooden boxes with hard benches where parishioners confess their sins to the priest sitting in the other wooden box. Of friends confessing secrets that remain between them, things not meant to be repeated. Journals that contain one's most private and personal thoughts. I think that it is a natural inclination for one to unburden the self with thoughts and feelings and emotions that weigh down the soul. It is recompense that is sought after; that leads one to the plush oversize chair in the protected realm of psychiatry.

I wonder about the things I keep inside, my own confessions, and my inability to acknowledge to another these things. I wonder if I have been able to admit to myself what I bury down into the core of my being. Is it fear of disappointing one that keeps me from saying I become unhappy in one place for too long? It is hard to see the ugliness of avoiding attachment and never allowing the self to admit love for another when the cause is unknown. It is a hard truth to admit to the self, a thing that makes one less than good in a world that strives for perfection.

I sit in the waning light of afternoon. With paper and pen I write my confessions, every thought and every hidden secret that

I can remember. When my mind becomes a blank space and my fingers hurt from the writing I hold the pages in my hand and I burn them, lighting an edge with my lighter. The pages curl and bend in the heat and the flame and when they burn close to my fingertips I drop them on the ground. The pieces burn out and flutter away in the wind.

I understand now how confession can be cathartic.

***

I dream. A city of ash and decay. Ash lies thick on the streets like fallen snow. I walk down the center of the street, my feet are bare and coated in the gray soot. There is no traffic, no cars or buses or taxis anywhere. There is only a heavy silence that makes me wonder if this is what it feels like to be deaf. Ash falls from the sky like large colorless snowflakes; a sky with the same gray as an impending storm.

Children walk slowly on the sidewalks, all of them barefoot and all of them wearing the same charcoal gray clothing. I wonder if they are lost, where they are going to, and why there are no adults. The children are not afraid or bewildered by the ash that covers the city. Ash falls on their hair and coats their clothing. They look like they have been born from fire instead of flesh.

A small girl stands in the street, her back to me. She is still, statuesque. I walk over to her, stop beside her. She stares straight ahead as if seeing something that I can't. Or watching the ash fall in layers over the buildings, turning the city into something dirty and gray and ugly. The girl doesn't move, doesn't blink. Her shallow breathing is the only sign that she is not a figment of my imagination. We don't speak.

Minutes pass. The child holds out her hand as if for me to take it, she is still looking straight ahead. I take her hand. She reaches up with her other hand, pointing down the street. I turn my head to see what it is she points at; there is nothing except for the falling ash and soot. When I turn back to the girl she is gone without even a footprint in the soot as evidence that she was real. The ash falls around me like snow. I am alone.

***

Two mirrors and my camera. These are the objects I use for my next photo project. A mirror held parallel to another mirror, the camera set in between. I stand facing one while holding another over one side of my face. The effect is a reflection of a half that continues on seemingly to infinity. Half a curve of the lips. Half the nose. One eye gazing forward under one shaped eyebrow. A perfect reflection of self in the sense there is only part of an individual revealed to others, the other part is contained and only unveiled with the ones that share the most personal and intimate circle within a life. There is an illusion of more, of a depth unseen in the resulting photographs.

Abramovic made a performance video in 1997 in which she stands facing the camera, a close up with only head and shoulders visible. Her hair pulled back away from her face, her eyes direct and unblinking. She holds her hands with palms turned toward the self, fingertips touching. Her movements are so slow and controlled that it is almost imperceptible as she moves her hands up to cover her eyes. As she does so there is a play of light that changes the part of her accentuated in the foreground. In the end her image is nothing more than a silhouette. She called this piece Lost Souls.

An illusion of depth, an implication that there is more than what one sees. A revealing and a hiddenness that shifts with the changing of light. A reflection of a half that makes me wonder if it is truly possible to know an individual as a whole. Or is the knowing based on the pieces, the fragments, that are seen?

***

I watch the news coverage of wildfires burning. Homes being evacuated and soaked with water in an effort to save them. Flames engulf and devour as they move over the hills, a living breathing malevolent being that leaves destruction and burns scars into the land. Like a fingerprint of Mother Nature as she destroys and renews. The fires have been burning for days, crews working around the clock to dig trenches and contain and extinguish a force greater than the manpower. There is panic. A push for the mayor to declare a state of emergency.

I remember the dream I once had of fire. Of purification by fire. I think of nature and of climate change that has turned the threat of seasonal wildfires into a year-round concern. I think about the earth's ability to heal and nurture itself if humanity's interference wasn't so detrimental and punishing. Fire can be healthy. Fire can renew.

Fire burns away buildup of decaying underbrush and plants that prevent access to nutrients within the soil. Fire clears away dead organic material that chokes new growth of plants. Burned material releases nutrients back into the soil quicker than if matter had decayed slowly over time. Pinecones that fall to the ground are covered in a pitch that, when melted away by fire, releases the seeds contained within.

A restoration out of the ash. A purification by fire. Not unlike the way a heart is burned by grief and trauma and love and is strengthened in the process.

***

A train ride to the countryside. Backpacks packed with bottles of water and granola and dried fruit. Sandwiches for later. My camera. We make our way to a hiking trail that in the busy summer months will be crowded with tourists on vacation but now is mostly deserted. The trail is well-worn from the many years of heavy foot traffic and makes for easy walking as we make our way further from the road and away from all the distractions of the city.

It is quiet here. There is only the sound of footsteps on the hard packed dirt and our voices to disturb the stillness. Trees crowd in on both sides and I can smell the sweet pine scent carried on the breeze and the lingering smell of damp wood from a recent rainfall.

In places where undergrowth has grown thick over the trail he goes before me to clear the way and I follow in his wake. It feels natural and comforting to feel his hand in mine and I try to remember a time when being with someone had felt this easy. It is a feeling I have never known.

Three miles in the trail runs parallel to a river that is fed by a large rushing waterfall. The water gushes over boulders worn smooth over time and when standing near it, the sound fills the ears and blocks out all else. At the base is a clear pool where the water slows. The only way to get down to the water is to make the two story jump.

We rest, setting packs in the dirt and drinking our water. We watch the water falling and pooling, falling and pooling. It is the same mesmerized feeling one has when staring into a fire or listening to the sound of a metronome in the silence of a room.

I tell him I want to swim under the waterfall and feel the spray as the water cascades above me. He tells me there's no way down. That the water would be too cold. I smile in response and kiss him full on the mouth. I stand and strip off hiking shoes and socks. Pants and sweatshirt and T shirt. I stand in bra and underwear overlooking the water below.

I jump.

***

A gallery room; lights dimmed. An empty space. One hundred eight video images projected on the back wall, playing simultaneously. Each video is of a Tibetan monk or nun randomly chanting meditative prayers. A cacophony of sound not unlike standing below a waterfall. Abramovic pieced together the collection during a month long stay at a monastery and called this work 'At the Waterfall'. A display of solemn faces and shaved heads and maroon robes. Of voices filling the room with prayer.

I imagine standing alone in the empty space. Eyes closed and feeling the meditative energy. Ears filled with voices chanting in languages I can't understand. Letting their prayers wrap around me like a holy spell. Calming and spiritual and hypnotic. Like standing before a wall of water that rushes over rock and falls ceaselessly to the depths below. Knowing that this beautiful and wild place was carved by nature, a stunning work of art that could never be replicated by human hands. Because spirituality cannot be made, it can only be felt in the heart when the soul recognizes that it is in proximity of something sacred.

I stand, cold and breathless but fully alive in all my senses, below the waterfall. I close my eyes and feel the spray on my skin and I think that it is not unlike being sprinkled with holy water. I remember a photograph in my spiral bound collection of Abramovic standing on a boulder in front of a large waterfall in Brazil. She wore a long white robe and stood reverently with arms out and eyes closed in the spray, her hair and robe soaked through. I understand now how she felt in that moment, listening to the rush and fall of the water.

Because the soul recognizes when it is in the proximity of something sacred.

***

I wrap myself in a blanket on the chaise, one of those over size throws that is as soft as chenille. It is dark and raining hard outside. I listen to it drumming on the roof and pelting on the windowpanes. The sort of night reminiscent of seances and ghost stories and nightmares. Of movies and popcorn and snuggling close under a shared blanket.

An unopen collection of poetry rests on my lap, pages turned down at the corners to mark my favorite passages. I am distracted, my mind a restless wanderer. I think about him. The way I feel when I am with him. Strong, yet vulnerable. Independent, yet supported. Love, yet fear. Fear of love. Fear of an attachment that fosters the growth of rootedness.

This city is a place where I have stayed the longest. Where I have explored, experienced and grown in spirit. I have tasted the fruit of being ingrained into a place and a people. I know that I won't stay. I know I will feel that familiar pull to move on to other places and other people yet to be known. I know that it will hurt to leave him.

In 1980 Abramovic and her partner made a video performance filmed in the Netherlands. 'Timeless Point of View' showed Abramovic in a wooden rowboat in the middle of a lake. She moves away from the shore, becoming smaller and smaller, the lifting and dipping of the oars the only movement. The boat was wired with a sound device that transmitted the sound of her rowing and the slapping of waves against wooden boat to her partner who stood on the shore, watching her going.

It is this image that is vivid in my mind when I think about moving on to another city, another state, another new beginning. I see myself fading into the distance until all that remains is the echo of a self.

For now though, I am here.

***

The morning is clear and warm, last night's rain a fading memory as the sun reaches to touch the city. I head out early with my leather satchel of camera equipment, stopping at the café on the corner for a hot coffee to sip while waiting at the bus stop. I watch the hustle of the morning commute, stop and start with the changing lights, suits and uniforms passing by on the sidewalks as another work day commences.

The bus deposits me only a few streets away from where I'm headed. I feel like a tourist as I pay the fare for the skypod elevator that takes me up to the Observatory. I stand in an enclosed circular space with walls of thick paned windows that overlook the city from over a hundred stories above. I am struck by the intensity of the view, I stand at the window and take in the endless skyscrapers and concrete and brick buildings. Rays of sunlight catch on windows and glint off metal and I think of a diamond sparkling.

Beyond the sea of buildings and streets I can see the harbor and the open ocean and I remember my night spent on the beach listening to its waves.

I take out my camera and photograph the city. I capture the sun refracting off the water in the distance. The white smoke from the mills that drifts across the tops of buildings before dissipating. The bridges and highways on the perimeter. I make my way around the Observatory, photographing each angle. I change the lens and settings, refocus. I capture my reflection in the glass, the skyline spread out behind me.

A man about my age stands alone, gazing out at the view with hands in pockets. He sees me, gestures at my camera and comments that it is a beautiful city, isn't it. I agree, especially from this height. He tells me that he comes here several times a year for business. No matter how many times he has seen it, this view is breath taking each time. He asks if I have been here at night, when the city shines in the dark.

More beautiful than this.

I shake my head no, tell him that I am only passing through. I think about the words once they have been said, wonder if I can truthfully say that since I have been living here. If I don't plan to stay indefinitely does that constitute passing through? I look out the window again, contemplating what it would feel like to call this place home.

I wonder if there will ever be a place that feels like home or if I will always be the restless wanderer.

***

We stand in an empty room, windows open to let in the spring warmth. Old white sheets cover the hardwood flooring. A bucket of paint and two paint rollers to start transforming a guest room into a nursery. She has chosen a pale olive color for the walls, a soft gender neutral color. She tells me she has decided not to know the gender before the baby arrives, that the sex isn't important compared to who this tiny human will be.

I think about the not knowing as I roll paint over the wall. I wonder if there is less gender scripting in the unknown, less ascribing certain characteristics of gender biases that subconsciously take hold when one prepares to meet this life that has formed within their womb for so many months. I think about the inclination of a culture to assign all things pink as a feminine color with the lace and frills and everything sky blue as a masculine color. A cultural mindset that believes the importance of gender differences and their roles begin the day one is brought into this world.

My friend reflects out loud that she wants to think in practical terms for the baby and what is needed instead of purchasing impulsively based on ideas of the sex. She rolls another coat of paint and begins to spread it over the back wall. She talks about onesies and sleepers in favor of miniature designer clothes. About finding a secondhand crib and baby swing in favor of the more expensive new options.

We discuss the world of baby items and how out of proportion the marketing is for new parents, a push to believe that so many extraneous things are needed for baby to be happy and comfortable and safe and smart. We talk about the practical needs: bonding, love, attention, a calm environment that nurtures. The material isn't important compared to the natural. It is the natural that will determine who this tiny human will be.

***

I walk in the direction of the city park, camera bag over my shoulder and cup of tea in my hand. A baby bird knocked from its nest, small body broken and lifeless on the brick sidewalk. I kneel down to see up close the scrawny body and tiny head, the little eyes pinched closed in death. I photograph the tiny body. A memory that life is fragile and fleeting. Life is movement. Without movement of body, movement of mind, movement of spirit, a being cannot live. The body will atrophy, become nothing more than a heap of flesh and bone.

Year 1978, in New York. Abramovic and her partner performed a piece titled 'Charged Space' in a gallery room before an audience of art historians, curators and critics. The artists stood facing one another, hands held together. They move in a circular motion, faster and faster, hands clasped together as in the child's game of ring around the rosy. Like a planet spinning upon its axis. They let go of one another, their bodies flung apart. The artists stumble and fall, dizzy and disoriented. They get up, urged by the voice of Abramovic's partner repeating the word 'Move'. Each stumbles against walls, into the audience and falls to the floor, the artist repeatedly calling out the command to 'Move'.

The gallery room where Charged Space took place was one with art work displayed on the walls, the performance a contrast between stationary art and art as life. Because life is movement. Movement of body. Movement of mind. Movement of spirit.

***

The news covers a story of a long term care facility under investigation after reports of elder abuse and neglect. I am angered by the accusations that some residents were found to have uncared for wounds in their thin and delicate skin from lack of mobility. That those with advanced cases of dementia were often restrained to keep them from wandering.

I think about the elderly and a society that marginalizes its oldest population. A culture that is so driven by an illusion of eternal youth that the old in need of care are pushed to the sideline, mostly ignored and forgotten. I think about the lives these older ones have lived, the wars and depression and generational unrest they have witnessed and survived. The bodies that have known physical labor to support families, bodies that have birthed and fed babies, that have danced and known love. The hands that have held and caressed and mended, now pained and frail with age and arthritis. I think about the roads broken and paved that the old had begun for the generations to come, about all that can occur in a lifetime, and how at the end of a life one is met with neglect and a society that simply no longer cares.

I think about cultures that revere and respect the elderly as the wisest among a people. Places that know the ones who have lived the longest have learned the most about life, have gained the most insight and contain a wealth of wisdom wanting to be shared with the younger generations. Cultures that understand the contributions made to society throughout generations the younger did not experience, the care given to others that now need to be given in return.

I watch the news story and I wonder if a society chooses to ignore its history contained within the ones who lived it? What kind of future is being established for the ones yet to come?

***

I dream of wisdom wearing the flesh of a feminine body. A woman who has seen all and knows all there is. I see her at the harbor, standing on the docks as if waiting for the boats to come in with their cache of lobster. Her face is turned to the sea, her long hair blowing in the wind. I stand at a distance but she knows that I am here. She turns slightly so her face is in profile. She asks me why I continue to leave footprints in the sand that are easily washed away with the tides instead of a foundation of cement that will hold indefinitely. She tells me that the constant seeker will never find what it is one seeks until one stops the seeking. Only then does one find what was being sought.

I try to speak but my words are small stones that fall from my mouth and clatter across the wooden dock. I crouch, trying to gather the smooth round stones into my palm as if I have lost something precious.

When I stand again there are black and white butterflies fluttering and hovering all around Wisdom. She holds out a hand and one rests on her fingertips, wings folded and still. She says the butterflies are her messengers, her words carried on the fragile wings. She tells me that when I seek her knowledge that I only need to look for the black and white butterflies.

The stones grow warm in my hand, emanating a heat that threatens to burn my skin. Wisdom turns to face me fully now and she gestures to my closed fist. She tells me that my words are burning with questions. But the questions do not have easy answers.

I awaken before the dream comes to an end, leaving Wisdom and her butterflies in the depths of sleep.

***

We stand together in my kitchen, cooking dinner and drinking wine. I chop vegetables for salad while he stirs the pot of pasta and simmers the sauce. The room is aromatic with the smell of tomatoes and spices and garlic. I sip from my glass of white wine, chop peppers to toss into the salad bowl. I listen to him tell me about a meditation class he has been trying that helps with the stress and worry about his family who are still in Poland. It is Vipassana meditation, a Buddhist technique. I have not heard of this before; I ask him to tell me about it.

He lifts a spoon to his lips, tastes of the sauce and then adds more oregano. He tells me that Vipassana means 'insight'. This meditation is a practice of eliminating all distractions, of just focusing on the connection between mind and body. An awareness of the physical sensations. Of seeing things only as they are. A process of freeing the mind of thought. Decluttering the mind.

I like the idea of freedom from thought. An experience of just being. Of allowing the body to feel what it will. Not allowing judgment or worry or thoughts that distract to settle like sediment on a lake bottom. I think about the network of the mind, a filter between thinking and feelings, where thirty-five thoughts per minute flow through. That Vipassana is like a cleansing of the filter not unlike the unblocking of energy within the body through the process of Reiki.

I wash and peel carrots and I wonder if one can truly see things only as they are, without inference or predetermined judgments. Without thought at all.

Vipassana as a result of becoming free from the mind.

***

The Netherlands 1985. An hour long video performance done by Abramovic and her partner. Modus Vivendi is a focus on the body's primary movements: Standing, sitting, lying or walking. Dressed in black, Abramovic's partner lies on top of four cardboard boxes. Without movement he lists out loud the things he is planning to do: "Rising, falling, touching, intending, bending, sitting, standing." He rises to a sitting position, facing back to the audience, and then stands. As he walks toward a roll of brown paper hung on the wall he describes the movement of his legs as he does so. He unrolls the paper to reveal a skeleton drawing of Siamese twins. The artist continues to describe his movements as he returns to a lying position once more on the cardboard boxes.

Abramovic appears on the left, tied to a tree that stands beside her and draped in a large piece of green fabric. She is motionless, her gaze focused straight ahead. Abruptly, she throws her hands up in the air. The lights go out.

I think of Modus Vivendi as an outward expression of Vipassana. Freedom from thought and distraction, a complete focus on the movement of the body. Attention to the physical sensations the body experiences in movement. At the same time a connection of mind and body, a coexistence dependent on the other not unlike a Siamese twin.

"Touching. Bending. Rising. Falling." Modus Vivendi.

***

I wake to a sunlit room and an empty bed. He is gone, memories of the night and the indentation in the pillow next to me the only evidence of a night spent together.

I remain in bed a while longer, reluctant to leave its comfortable warmth. Reluctant to leave behind the night of food and laughter and conversation and touch. I want to stay with it a little longer and not have to face a new day just yet. I close my eyes again, replay the night before.

After a time I get up and shower, make a cup of coffee to awaken the senses. I head outside into the bright morning. Today is the farmers' market.

The city is busy and loud. A thick smog hangs over everything like a fog yet to burn off. I notice the chain link fences that enclose neighborhood yards. That surround schools. The tall buildings and skyscrapers that close in the open expanse of sky.

I walk the same sidewalks that I have walked every day and for the first time I feel caged in. I feel a tightness in my chest like the way one feels in claustrophobic places. Like it's hard to breathe here.

A few blocks from where I live there is an outdoor magazine and newspaper stand. I stop to read the headlines on the front page of the paper. It is the atlas at the bottom that draws my attention. I pick it up and leaf through the pages, my fingers trailing over the thin lines mapping directions to other places like mapping a destination to freedom.

A butterfly flutters around the papers and magazines. Hovers and comes to rest on the edge of the metal stand. Black body with white wings, black smudge tracing around the edges. A black and white butterfly. I remember my dream of Wisdom and her butterflies.

This is how I know.

***

A week is how long it takes. To pay the last of the rent. To pack only what is most important and to pawn what someone else might find worthy. To make a drop off at the Salvation Army. In the end a life is reduced to one suitcase and one backpack of belongings.

A bus ticket to nowhere and anywhere.
I sit in the window of the bus, watching the city roll away. I think of the people I have known here and the memories that I will carry with me like photographs taken with the heart. The fisherman at the harbor, a nomad and fellow restless wanderer. The homeless teenager. The displaced persons living in a city park. My pregnant friend. Our last time spent together and an emotional goodbye. And him. The most difficult to leave. There is peace in the leaving. This is how I know.

***

In March 1988 Abramovic and her partner, who had also been her lover for many years as they worked and lived together, ended their relationship. Before going their separate ways the pair decided to walk the entire length of the Great Wall of China. They would begin the journey at opposite ends and meet in the middle. A final performance together they called 'The Lovers'.

Abramovic began her walk near the Bohai Sea. She slept in nearby villages and hostels along the way.

Her partner began his trek in the Gobi Desert. He crossed the Yellow River by raft and slept outside or in nearby villages.

Ninety days and a combined thirteen thousand one hundred seventy-one miles later the artists met among a series of temples built during the Ming dynasty. Their tearful meeting and parting was captured on video and in pictures that tugged at heart strings around the globe.

A beautiful goodbye.

CPSIA information can be obtained
at www.ICGtesting.com
Printed in the USA
BVHW030513060723
666781BV00007B/264